I tore ~~out of bed, and with one heave~~ pulled the curtains right back.

Nothing there, of course.

Only there was something floating right outside my window.

A hand.

A skeletal hand dripping with blood.

The hand wriggled and twisted. And before I knew it, a second hand was there.

It too was covered in blood and writhed about madly. I could just about make out a shape behind the hands as well. But it was very misty and unclear. All I could really see was those hands. It was as if they were trying to send me a message. And I had to know what it was. I found myself moving even closer until my face was right up against the glass.

That's when the message crept into my head: 'Let me in. You must let me in . . .'

How many Pete Johnson books have you read?

Vampire Titles
THE VAMPIRE BLOG
Winner of THE BRILLIANT BOOK AWARD
'Pete Johnson's approach to the very fashionable theme of vampires was very refreshing with lots of humour thrown in but still tension and scary bits – the characters are well designed and believable' *Library Mice Review*

THE VAMPIRE HUNTERS
'Another fantastically written book by Pete Johnson. Packed full of adventure, comedy, laughs, intriguing characters and a little bit of blood. This is a must read' *Scribbler*

Thrillers
AVENGER
Winner of the 2006 Sheffield Children's Book Award, best shorter novel
Winner of the 2005 West Sussex Children's Book Award
'Brilliant' *Sunday Express*

THE CREEPER
'Explores the subtle power of the imagination' *Books for Keeps*

EYES OF THE ALIEN
'Very readable with a skilful plot' *Observer*

THE FRIGHTENERS
'Prepare to be thoroughly spooked' *Daily Mail*

THE GHOST DOG
Winner of the 1997 Young Telegraph / Fully Booked Award
'Incredibly enjoyable' *Books for Keeps*

TRAITOR
'Fast-paced and energetic' *The Bookseller*

PHANTOM FEAR
Includes:
MY FRIEND'S A WEREWOLF *and* THE PHANTOM THIEF

Funny Stories
THE BAD SPY'S GUIDE
Shortlisted for the 2007 Blue Peter Book Award, Book I Couldn't Put Down category
'This book grabs you from the first page (5 stars)' *Sunday Express*

HELP! I'M A CLASSROOM GAMBLER
Winner of the 2007 Leicester Our Best Book Award
'A real romp of a read that will leave readers ravenous for more' *Achuka*

HOW TO GET FAMOUS
Winner of the Sheffield Community Libraries Prize

HOW TO TRAIN YOUR PARENTS
'Makes you laugh out loud' *Sunday Times*

RESCUING DAD
'Most buoyant, funny and optimistic' *Carousel*

THE TV TIME TRAVELLERS
'Another great humorous book from critically acclaimed Pete Johnson' *Literacy Times*

TRUST ME, I'M A TROUBLEMAKER
Winner of the 2006 Calderdale Children's Book of the Year (Upper Primary)

THE VAMPIRE FIGHTERS

Pete Johnson

CORGI YEARLING BOOKS

THE VAMPIRE FIGHTERS
A CORGI YEARLING BOOK 978 0 440 86940 5

First published in Great Britain by Corgi Yearling,
an imprint of Random House Children's Publishers UK
A Random House Group Company

This edition published 2012

1 3 5 7 9 10 8 6 4 2

Text copyright © Pete Johnson, 2012

The right of Pete Johnson to be identified as the author of this work has been
asserted in accordance with the Copyright, Designs and Patents Act 1988.

The Random House Group Limited supports the Forest Stewardship Council
(FSC®), the leading international forest certification organization. Our
books carrying the FSC label are printed on FSC®-certified paper. FSC is
the only forest certification scheme endorsed by the leading environmental
organizations, including Greenpeace. Our paper procurement policy can be
found at www.randomhouse.co.uk/environment.

MIX
Paper from
responsible sources
FSC® C016897

Set in Century Schoolbook 12.5/16pt by Falcon Oast Graphic Art Ltd

Corgi Yearling Books are published by Random House
Children's Publishers UK, 61–63 Uxbridge Road, London W5 5SA

www.kidsatrandomhouse.co.uk
www.totallyrandombooks.co.uk
www.randomhouse.co.uk

Addresses for companies within The Random House Group Limited can be
found at: www.randomhouse.co.uk/offices.htm

THE RANDOM HOUSE GROUP Limited Reg. No. 954009

A CIP catalogue record for this book is available from the British Library.

Printed and bound by CPI Group (UK) Ltd, Croydon, CR0 4YY

This book is dedicated to all the reading groups I've met – or who have contacted me. Your strong feelings about what happens next to Marcus, Tallulah and Gracie have inspired me. I hope you approve of what does happen to them!

PROLOGUE

Something moved in the darkness.

Something to be feared, always.

The Blood Ghost.

That's what they've started calling it. It's all over my local radio. I bet it will have its own Facebook page soon.

A woman glimpsed it first on New Year's Eve. It was a dusty-grey morning and she was rushing off to the local shop. She was walking quickly down the lane where she lived when she heard an urgent, high-pitched screech.

'Like a really angry parrot,' was her description of it. She peered up into the sky, half expecting to see a bird fluttering about. But instead a figure came floating towards her.

Hard to make out much about him as it was

1

so shadowy and loomed dazzlingly high above her. All she could really see was its hands. They were just like the hands of a skeleton, very long and spindly and they seemed to be beckoning her forward. Dripping off them was something that made her whole body shudder with horror – blood.

Those skeletal blood-soaked hands writhed and twisted in front of her. She wanted to run away from them. But the hands seemed to be casting a terrible spell over her. And instead, she was frozen to the spot.

Then, as fast as a striking cobra, one of the hands swooped at her. There was a huge rush of air, and just for a moment she caught a glimpse of its deathly, pale face. And it terrified her. Then it displayed all its teeth at her. It was the most horrific smile she'd ever seen, because its dark eyes were completely blank and lifeless.

She felt as if this awful, dead creature was trying to pull her towards it and carry her away. And all her strength seemed to have drained from her body. Then she felt her knees buckle. She couldn't stop herself falling onto the ground while it loomed right over her.

She'd almost passed out when she heard quick, urgent footsteps tearing towards her. Afterwards she said how lucky it was that her husband had realized she'd forgotten her purse and come after her. 'I say lucky,' she said, 'yet actually, what could it have done – except scare me? It was only a very nasty ghost.'

But it wasn't only a ghost. I knew exactly what it was too.

And I so wished I didn't.

CHAPTER ONE

Three days earlier
Monday 29 December

9.30 a.m.

Hi, blog.

I'm back.

Remember me? Marcus – or Weirdo.

I was totally normal until three months ago, when I turned thirteen. On the night of my birthday my parents, ever so casually, announced that they were half-vampires and that I was about to start transforming into one too.

I was still trying to get my head around that newsflash when a white fang slammed itself into my mouth – and stayed there for a couple of days. And that was just the start. After that I was poisoned by a pizza (it had garlic in it) and I got a craving for blood when I was at the cinema on a blind date. It did not go well.

Still, you say it must be cool being a half-vampire.

Do you want to know the truth? It totally is not. In fact, it's all hiding and hassle. Worst of all, you feel separate and odd and different to everyone else. It's as if I'm permanently freaky. I can't tell you how much I hate that.

But come on, surely there must be some highlights? Yeah, OK, here they are – I can stay up until 3 a.m. every night. And sometimes I go flitting – that's when I transform into a bat and can fly about for – well, over half an hour last night.

Back in November I acquired a special power too. For a few hours I could beam out my thoughts to the only other teenage half-vampire I know – a dead cool and funny girl called Gracie. I was able to pick up her thoughts too.

Now that was awesome. Especially as just a few half-vampires have a strong special power – only a tiny number would be able to do telepathy, for instance. In fact, I could only do it for a few hours. But a special power was supposed to zoom back to me – only permanently this time. It wouldn't necessarily mean I could do telepathy again, although a power that strong would be fantastic. It might be anything – being extra-strong or discovering I could suddenly run really fast. So I was excited – but nowhere near as excited as my parents.

And we all waited – and waited – for a special power to land on me again. And stay this time.

We're still waiting.

'We've just got to be patient,' Dad kept saying, acting all cheerful to my face. But I also heard him and Mum whispering away about how it really should have manifested itself by Christmas.

And now I've just had a total bombshell.

You're not going to believe this, blog. I can hardly believe it myself. But at the time of year when every school in the country – in fact, in the *world* – is closed, I've got to go back to school tomorrow. Only not my usual school. No, I'm being packed off on a special two-day crash course for half-vampires 'in my situation' at a place called Fangstone House.

'It's to help you bring out your special power,' said Mum.

'Absolutely and definitely not,' I said. 'I go to school enough. Right now I just need to relax.'

'We agree,' said Mum unexpectedly.

'So what are we arguing about?' I asked.

'We're not arguing, we're discussing,' said Dad. 'And we agree you need to relax. We just think you'll do that better at Fangstone House.'

Have you ever heard of anything more insane in your whole life? I tried to explain to them just how mad this plan was. But they wouldn't listen.

'We've discussed this enough now,' said Mum suddenly. 'We've made up our minds, so that's an end to it.'

'My opinion doesn't count then,' I said.

'Of course it does, and we've let you have your say,' said Mum, 'but we are your parents.'

It so annoys me when they say that. They know they've lost the argument so they just resort to – 'We are your parents, and we know best.'

Tuesday 30 December

10.45 a.m.

They've finally told me where Fangstone House is. It's in London, just off Covent Garden, down a road called Gore(!) Avenue. Apparently, it's a favourite place for half-vampires, although no human can ever know that, of course.

Dad's spoken to Dr Chaney, who runs things. My overnight bag is packed. And we're off any second. I can't wait.

10.47 a.m.

Yes, I can.

6.45 p.m.

I'm now writing to you from my cell – oops, I mean my room. Gore Avenue was full of big posh houses (some half-vampires must be loaded) and Fangstone House was right at the end. There was a little sign outside which just said *Dr Chaney*.

Mum pressed the doorbell and a woman with a dead fierce expression bustled to the door. She'd have made a great bouncer. There was a bit of whispering between her and my parents, which irritated me. I'm not six. Then the Bouncer announced that my parents could leave me here now and she'd ring when I was ready to be collected.

I was more than a bit sorry to see my parents go. But of course I didn't let on, as I was also very, very annoyed with them.

Then the Bouncer, breathing noisily like a mad bull, escorted me into a room which was a bit like a dentist's waiting room. Only nowhere near so cheerful. Two boys and one girl were sitting bolt upright on posh chairs. They looked as if they were about to sit the world's toughest exam.

'Hey, this is fun, isn't it?' I said. 'I'm Marcus, if you want to know. And you really should. So, who are you?'

But before anyone could reply, this deep, solemn voice declared, 'There is no point in finding out people's names. You won't be here long enough for that.' A stern-faced man was standing very still in the doorway with his arms folded. He was tall and quite old, with a long pointy beard. He was dressed in a black suit and looked more like an undertaker than a headmaster. This was Dr Chaney.

He said, 'We have a one hundred per cent success rate in helping half-vampires tease out their special powers. So if you trust us and work with us, all will be well. And I hope your stay here will be very short and highly successful. Now I am going to entrust you to your personal tutor, who is waiting for you in your tutorial rooms. Miss Ramsay will escort you there first, Marcus.'

The Bouncer led me to a room right at the end of a long corridor. I was told to knock on the door and walk straight in. I did, expecting to see tables and chairs, but it was empty save for a phone on the wall, and not like a normal classroom at all. It was also totally deserted. And I was thinking, *Why have they pushed me in here?* And, *I really want to go home now*, when I realized I wasn't alone at all. Someone else was there – lying on a large yellow roll mat on the floor.

A youngish woman beamed up at me, said her name was Tara and she was very pleased to meet me. She was wearing a multi-coloured top, green trousers and pink trainers. She looked as if she'd escaped from a TV show for two-year-olds. Then she asked me what I'd like most in the world.

'Right now,' I said, 'to emigrate.'

Amazingly, that wasn't the right answer. I should have said what I most wanted was to develop my own special half-vampire power. Tara said this special power was trying to break through but couldn't because I'd put up an invisible wall around myself.

'Not meaning to be rude, Tara,' I said to the figure still lying on the floor, 'but that's total rubbish. I was up for the special power but it just hasn't happened yet.'

'But do you know why?' said Tara, and without waiting for me to reply she went on, 'Because you need unblocking.'

'I'm not a drain,' I muttered.

Then I had to lie down next to her on an 'especially soothing' roll mat, which was waiting for me. She told me my half-vampire self was like my shadow self, which I kept pushing away from me. 'But' – and she got all excited then – 'there's gold inside that shadow self, which you'll find when you befriend it.'

After which she said I had to greet my half-vampire self by stretching my hand out and shouting, 'Hi there, half-vampire self, you're very welcome.'

'Really?' I said.

'Yes, please.'

'How about if I do it on my own later?'

'No, now please.'

So there I was, lying on the floor next to a total stranger – and chatting to my hand. I murmured very quietly, 'Hi there, half-vampire self, you're very welcome,' while feeling totally, totally stupid.

'You can do much better than that,' she said. 'And you will.'

Two centuries later I was allowed to stop talking to my hand and instead I had to chant, 'Hey, I'm a really great half-vampire, so happy with everything.' After which Tara really expected I'd feel a tingling in my hands – this would be the first sign my special power was breaking through.

She kept asking if I was sure I couldn't feel the tiniest tingle. And when I confirmed my tingle-free situation, this caused a bit of a downer in the general atmosphere. Tara even stopped smiling for five seconds. But then she said determinedly, 'We'll just have to carry on unblocking tomorrow.' Then she got up and started talking into a phone. 'Hello, Miss Ramsay. Alas, no breakthrough yet but we're stopping now. So will you show Marcus to his room, please . . . What? Oh, really? Well, that's excellent news. Bye.'

'What's excellent news?' I asked.

Tara didn't seem at all keen to tell me, and then said very quietly, 'Two of the students you met are now ready to go home.'

'So their special power has come through already.'

'That's right, but it's not a competition. And we shan't be downhearted. A breakthrough could happen at any moment, couldn't it?'

'If you say so,' I muttered. I was just so fed up with the whole business.

'A meal will be waiting for you in

your room. Your parents said you didn't have any special dietary requirements.'

'No, except for barbecue hula hoops, that's a big dietary requirement. And jelly babies, just passionate about them. And HP sauce . . .' I babbled on until the ever-uncheerful Bouncer showed me to my room.

How can I describe it to you? It was a delightful shade of vomit yellow. It had a bed and a table in it (on which was perched a deeply unappetizing salad) and that was it, except for a bathroom and loo which had obviously been designed for a midget elf. Anyway, I'm not allowed to leave this room again tonight – and just to make sure I don't, it's firmly locked. They think the silence will calm and centre me. But actually, I hate those silences which just stretch on and on.

Still, at least I can text Gracie (the only person I can ever tell about this place). She's as angry as me that I'm here.

She texted:

It just feels as if you're in a massive detention.

I texted back:

That's exactly how it feels and any resemblance my room has to a prison cell is purely intentional.

9.35 p.m.
Gracie is now bombarding me with silly texts like:

Do you get a prize for the weirdest special power?

She alone is keeping me sane.

Wednesday 31 December

8.30 a.m.
I was woken up by the Bouncer for breakfast. My jaw nearly fell off when I saw what I was being served up – lumpy porridge. Apparently it's bursting with vitamins. It's certainly not bursting with flavour. Even Oliver Twist would have refused seconds.

12.50 p.m.

I've now completed four hours of intensive relaxation exercises with Tara. We've done deep breathing, followed by not-so-deep breathing and chanting. And I don't think I've ever felt so unrelaxed.

1.20 p.m.

Just heard that the other student who came here with me has also left armed with his special power. So now there's just me, still unblocked.

8.15 p.m.

Well, blog, I'm back home. And remember I told you Fangstone House has always had a one hundred per cent success rate? Well, I've totally messed up their statistics. I'm sort of chuffed about that. Anyway, late this afternoon they gave up on me and sent for my parents.

Tara gave them a list of exercises I must perform every night. 'If Marcus really gets stuck in, I'm sure wonderful things could still start to happen,' she said. Tara also gave me her phone number if ever I wanted to talk over anything. This seemed highly unlikely, but I put it on my mobile anyway.

My parents were trying to act all cheerful in the car. But once I noticed Dad take hold of Mum's hand in a sloppy sort of way. And Mum whispered, 'No, no, I'm all right. I haven't given up hope.'

Thursday 1 January: New Year's Day

12.30 a.m.

Mum, Dad and I toasted in the New Year with a small glass of blood. Then Dad said, 'I've got another toast now – to Marcus's special power. It's certainly taking its time.' Quick glance at Mum here. 'But it will be worth waiting for when it finally appears.'

Actually, I'm convinced my special power is a no-show. Fangstone House wouldn't have chucked me out if there was the remotest chance of it making an appearance. And yeah, all right, I am a little bit gutted about that. I'd like to have been a suave superhero. Who wouldn't? Plus, I'd have loved to have really blown my parents' socks off – and not disappointed them yet again.

But a superhero isn't really me. It never was. And deep down I always knew that. So I don't care any more. I truly, honestly don't.

I've even made a New Year's Resolution. Here it is. Not only will I refuse to go on any more crash courses, but I shan't ever think about my special power again.

Instead, I'm going to concentrate on something much more important – girls.

I got a text yesterday from Joel, my best mate, saying that Katie, his girlfriend, was dropping round his house on New Year's Eve. They've been going out together for a record-breaking six weeks now. And I'm chuffed for him. Of course I am. But news like that makes you think. And yeah, you guessed it, I'm pretty envious too (understatement).

Especially as I'm single right now. An astonishing fact when you consider my immense charm and good looks and overall modesty. Really I should be some sort of international girl magnet. Actually, girls do sort of like me. Well, I can make them laugh.

Except the one I really fancy – Tallulah.

I've decided she's a total stunner. But you won't find a boy in my class who'll agree with me.

And yeah, I know Tallulah can be very fierce and bad-tempered – and that's when she's in a good mood. You really wouldn't want to get on the wrong side of her. She also never wears a scrap of makeup and doesn't ever dress up either. But I sort of admire that about her. And she's still dead pretty, with her heart-shaped face and huge eyes that can look right into you.

Lastly, but firstly really – Tallulah's obsessed with vampires. She's so mad about them she even started up her own website, **Vampira,** as she believed that vampires lurk right here in Great Walden.

Now I have inside information on this, so I can tell you that humans have nothing to fear from my very distant relatives, despite what you might have read in books. You see, it is animal blood that vampires like, not human blood (too sour). Only now there's a new sect – the deadly vampires – who believe that human blood, despite its foul taste, can give them incredible new powers. They don't care how much of it they take either.

These deadly vampires are truly to be feared – by everyone. And last November one moved here and started attacking innocent humans until Tallulah – ably assisted by yours truly – caught it.

Impressed? My parents weren't. No. They gave me a massive rollicking. You see, I had put the secret identity of half-vampires in danger. And the first and most important rule of being a half-vampire is: no human must ever discover our true nature. And I totally get that. For if people discovered there were half-vampires living in their road it would scare the living daylights out of them – even though you couldn't find a more peace-loving species than us. So my parents made me promise I'd keep away from vampires, deadly vampires – and Tallulah.

But meanwhile, Tallulah was meeting up with this vampire hunter called Giles. He believed more deadly vampires were on their way to Great Walden, and they must be stopped. So he enlisted Tallulah as a vampire fighter.

The next bit of my story is embarrassing and I don't come out of it well. So I'm going to get it over with quickly. Tallulah tried to enlist me as a vampire fighter too. And I broke my promise to my parents – and agreed. Why on earth did I do that?

Well, you see, Tallulah confided in me how she'd caught this very nasty bug while on holiday. And she just can't shake it off either. So I felt sorry for her. And don't forget, I do like her.

But right away I knew I'd made a very bad decision.

After that, though, I got flu and so did Tallulah. Giles even ended up in hospital with it. So absolutely nothing has happened for weeks.

I did send Tallulah some texts, though. And I really thought she and I had bonded, so I waited and waited for her to reply. She took ages even to do that. And when she finally did they were so frost-bitten, so nothing, that I immediately un-enlisted myself from any vampire fighting. I haven't told Tallulah yet. Well, I might not even have to, as it all seems to have fizzled out anyway.

And as for me ever going out with her, that's just another dream, like me having special powers or being an international girl magnet.

It'll never happen.

I totally see that now.

12.30 p.m.

Just had a text from Tallulah. Here's what it said:

Totally urgent. Giles just sent me a text. Meet me at the bus shelter outside Giles's house at 7 p.m. tonight. I dare not give any more information by text or phone – but listen to the local radio news. It's really started. And it's brilliant!

CHAPTER TWO

Thursday 1 January

1.15 p.m.

So there I was in my bedroom, listening to the local radio. Tons of deadly dull stuff first, with some politician yakking on about his hopes for the New Year. I just hoped he'd stop talking.

But then the announcer said with a little chuckle in his voice, 'And now – how about a spooky story for New Year's Day? Meet "the Blood Ghost".'

For the next few minutes a woman called Marilyn told us what she'd seen, while a chill crept right down my spine. I immediately saw the truth behind her 'ghost' story. A deadly vampire had transformed itself into a ghostly form, used its hands to hypnotize its victim and then returned to its normal bat-like form to drain its victim of blood. And Marilyn hadn't fainted with shock as she thought, but because so much of her blood had been drunk. It was just very lucky her husband turned up when he did.

The only thing which didn't quite fit with it being a deadly vampire was the timing of the attack. I'd never heard of a vampire operating in the daytime before.

I was still pondering this when I heard a creak behind me. I whirled round to see both my parents. They'd been there for a while too, listening to the story of the Blood Ghost.

And I could just tell from the uneasy look in their eyes that they'd guessed what the Blood Ghost really was too. Not that they'd say anything aloud. They never spoke about vampires during the day and hardly even at night either. Vampires were our deeply dodgy, distant relatives. So it was easier to pretend they weren't anything to do with us.

My mum and dad hadn't forgotten – or forgiven me for tracking down a deadly vampire in Great Walden either. And I knew the last thing they'd want would be for me to investigate the Blood Ghost now.

'You don't normally listen to this radio channel,' Mum said. She sounded suspicious.

'Oh, I was just flicking about,' I said as casually as I could, with both my parents eyeballing me. I gabbled on, 'That woman is enjoying her fifteen minutes of fame. But it's probably all made up.'

'Oh, I'm sure it is,' said Dad slowly. But he didn't really believe that.

And neither did I.

2.30 p.m.

I've been listening to more about the Blood Ghost. But I had the radio on really low and all the time I was watching out for my parents. For if they knew I was taking all this interest in it – well, their suspicions would be sky-high. But anyway, it wasn't very interesting. A so-called expert on ghosts was just nattering away. He thought Marilyn had seen a figure from the past. Maybe someone who'd died on this spot long ago.

If only that were true.

2.45 p.m.

I'm writing a text to Tallulah telling her I'm not going with her to see Giles tonight. Also that I'm resigning from the mission, because . . . well, I just don't like socializing with deadly vampires.

2.47 p.m.

Text all written now. Of course, I'll never actually send it.

2.49 p.m.

Well, it's cowardly – and rude – to tell Tallulah this news by text, isn't it?

6.15 p.m.

In the kitchen and just finishing my beetroot sandwiches (a favourite half-vampire snack) when Mum and Dad crashed down beside me.

'We've got a surprise for you,' said Dad.

'An exciting surprise,' said Mum.

Now, my parents' idea of something exciting would be a visit to the local pencil museum so I managed to contain my enthusiasm. 'What is it, then?' I asked. 'And it hasn't got anything to do with Fangstone House, has it?'

'No, no – well, not really,' said Mum, beaming away at me. 'It's those relaxation exercises Tara gave you to do. You're not going to have to do them on your own. We'll join in with you.'

'Starting tonight,' said Dad. 'We'll really get stuck in.'

This wasn't a surprise, it was a nightmare. I couldn't think of anything worse than all three of us lying on the floor chanting all that rubbish. And it was a total waste of time.

But I decided to be kind and let my parents down lightly. 'That sounds like brilliant fun, and I hate to miss it, but I'm off out tonight. Still, if you two want to start without me that's fine.'

'Where are you going?' demanded Mum.

Of course, I didn't dare tell them that. 'Oh, just out,' I said vaguely.

'Actually, Marcus, we'd really rather you didn't go out tonight,' said Mum.

'Why?' I asked at once.

'No particular reason.'

But I knew this sighting of the Blood Ghost had unnerved them.

'I'm only going round to Joel's house,' I lied.

'You can see Joel another night,' said Dad.

'No, I can't,' I said, 'because he's got to talk to me ever so urgently about a . . .' I frantically tried to think of something. In the end I unleashed two of the most powerful words I know: 'Personal problem.'

Here's a tip for you now, blog. If ever you're in trouble, say, for not handing in your homework, all you've got to do is fix the teacher with a solemn stare and say very quietly, 'I'm very sorry, but I couldn't complete the homework because of . . . a personal problem.'

Then just watch your teachers back away instantly. Those two words have never let me down yet – and they didn't tonight. Dad began, 'Well, I suppose if Joel really needs to talk over something with you . . .'

'Oh, he really does,' I said in a low, husky tone.

'But has it got to be tonight?' asked Mum.

I nodded my head ever so gravely.

So now they've agreed I can go out tonight.

But I've still got to be home by ten o'clock for those relaxation exercises we're going to do as a family. Yuck!

6.50 p.m.

I called at Joel's house first. In the kitchen, after he'd told me all about his evening with Katie the night before (now I'm even *more* envious), I said to him, 'My mum and dad think you've got a personal problem.'

'Why?'

'Because I told them you have.'

'Cheers for that.'

'And if they should ring, I'm helping you sort it all out. But really . . . I'm seeing a girl.'

'Excellent. What's her name?'

'Tallulah.'

'Your taste doesn't improve.'

'No, I'm seeing her to tell her we're finished. Not that we ever really started.'

'So why all the cloak-and-dagger stuff?'

'My parents don't like her.'

'You amaze me.'

As I was leaving, Joel whispered, 'I was about to say, have a good time, but then I remembered who you're seeing.'

I ran like a loon all the way to the bus shelter outside Giles's house in Priestly Drive. I was only a few minutes late. But no one was waiting. Tallulah must have gone on without me. What a colossal cheek, especially after I'd made all this effort . . . but then I spotted a small figure asleep in the corner of the shelter.

And my heart gave a jolt – just as it used to when I discovered I'd forgotten my games kit or I couldn't answer any of the questions in an exam. Only now it was a girl causing this. Is that a sign I'm maturing – or am I just turning horribly soppy? Not really sure.

Anyway, Tallulah's head was leaning sideways against the seat. She looked very beautiful but as pale as chalk.

If I'd found Joel or another mate asleep I'd just have shouted, 'Hey, stupid face!' down his ear. But I decided Tallulah deserved something a bit more subtle. So I said, 'Hey, Tallulah, it's Marcus, your favourite guy in the entire universe.' No reaction. I said it again, much louder. Still nothing. Finally I

31

whispered, 'Blood Ghost.' Her eyes shot open then all right.

'You've got to stop dreaming about me,' I said.

'I wasn't asleep,' she snapped, blinking up at me.

'Best impression of someone not sleeping I've ever seen.'

She jumped up. 'You're late. Where have you been?'

'Watching you not sleeping.' Then, keen to strike a friendlier note, 'So, how was your Christmas? Give me all the hairy details.'

'I don't do Christmas,' said Tallulah flatly, 'because I'm allergic to my family. Well, they hate me so I hate them.'

'I'm sure they don't actually hate you.'

'Oh, they do, and I can understand it really. My brother and sister are so happy, shiny and perfect and never any trouble. And then there's me, the total opposite. No wonder I have rows with them every minute of every hour of the day.'

I knew Tallulah had this massive grudge against her family (and many other people too, actually). But she was exaggerating now, wasn't she? Then I had to add, 'Cheers for all those amazing texts you never sent me.'

'Well, I've been in such a bad mood.'

'You? Never.'

'This stupid illness has made me tired and grumpy all the time and I . . . wait, why are we talking about boring stuff like that when there's the Blood Ghost to deal with? Which is really a deadly vampire – it's got to be. And this is what we've been waiting for, isn't it?'

It really wasn't, but I liked the 'we'. Tallulah just assumed I was as keen on this whole mission as she was. So this wasn't the moment to inform her that I was bailing out. And I suppose I was a tiny bit curious as to what Giles was going to tell us.

7.28 p.m.

We rang and rang on Giles's doorbell, but he didn't answer.

'I don't believe it,' said Tallulah. 'He said it was really urgent. So where is he? Something's wrong.'

I tried to look concerned. 'Maybe he's found out it wasn't a deadly vampire, after all. Or perhaps he's just got other stuff to do.'

I started to walk away. 'Shall we go for a walk and—'

'His door's not closed properly,' interrupted Tallulah. 'Do you think he meant us to just go in?'

'No,' I began, but Tallulah had already dashed inside. I suppose I'd better go after her.

8.30 p.m.

The first shock of the night was when we stepped inside Giles's house.

CHAPTER THREE

Thursday 1 January

8.30 p.m. (cont'd)

Tallulah darted into the kitchen. 'He's probably in here,' she said.

But he wasn't.

'Come on, Giles, where are you hiding?' I demanded, strolling into another room. Apart from a tottering pile of books on a table, this had an odd, unlived-in feel about it. I remembered suddenly that this was exactly how Giles's house had seemed the first time I'd seen it. Then I swerved to a sudden stop and let out a gasp loud enough for Tallulah to hear.

'What?' she called.

'Tallulah, just stay where you are. Don't move.'

'What is it? Tell me!' cried Tallulah.

'It's Giles, he's lying spread-eagled across the carpet.'

'Oh no!'

'No, not really,' I said, strolling out of the room. 'Joke.'

Tallulah opened her mouth to say something highly indignant, but instead a voice demanded, 'What are you doing in here?' A voice which seemed to have just risen up out of the air. Then we realized someone was standing on the stairs.

Only it wasn't Giles.

This man tripped quickly down the stairs towards us. He was extremely tall and quite young, probably in his twenties. So much younger than Giles.

'We rang for ages,' said Tallulah. 'And then we saw it was open.'

'I'm so absent-minded it isn't true,' said the man, waving an ornate walking stick at us. 'But I do know who you are. You're . . .'

'Tallulah and Marcus,' prompted Tallulah.

'Of course,' he said.

'And who are you?' I asked.

'I'm Giles's nephew, Cyril. And I've been waiting for you.'

'Actually,' I said, 'it was Giles we were expecting to see. He sent Tallulah a text.'

'No, he didn't,' said Cyril. 'I sent it. Here, come and join me upstairs in the study and I'll explain. You two have a busy time ahead of you.' Then, without another word he disappeared upstairs again.

'We've no proof he is Giles's nephew,' I hissed. 'He could even be the deadly vampire luring us into a trap.'

'That's true,' said Tallulah, not seemingly very bothered by this possibility. 'But the front door's still open so we'll just have to run for our lives.'

We followed him into a creepy room at the top of the stairs. It was full of old furniture – there was even a massive grandfather clock in the corner. There were also shelves and shelves of books too, and every one seemed to be about vampires and the supernatural.

But it was the pictures on the walls that were so eerie. They were all of vampires too. Crouched figures ready to spring at some unsuspecting victim. Or with massive stakes through their heart. But there was one picture which I kept looking at even though I really didn't want to. It was of this woman screaming because something had seized hold of her ankle . . . a skeletal hand that seemed to have just pushed its way through the earth. And it was totally covered in blood.

'Now this is what I call a decent room,' said Tallulah, obviously loving the way vampires seemed to swirl round us in every corner.

Cyril was standing at the end of the room, leaning lightly on the stick and watching us with a faintly amused air. There was just one dim light on in this room but I could see him a bit clearer now. He had a very long face; in fact he looked more than a bit like a horse. And his teeth hung out of his mouth as if he was halfway through a sneeze. He was wearing a very old-fashioned suit with a matching blue handkerchief peeping out the top pocket. If he'd suddenly pulled out a pocket watch and a chain I wouldn't have been very surprised.

'This room,' he announced, 'is where my Uncle Giles lives.'

'But where exactly is he?' I asked.

'Uncle Giles is still convalescing from his flu and is not well enough to come home yet. So he has left me in charge.'

'You say that,' I said, 'but you could be anyone.'

'I could be, but I'm not,' said Cyril. 'Still, Uncle Giles said you might raise this. So here's a note from him explaining the situation.' He waved a piece of paper in front us which said, *This is to introduce my nephew, Cyril . . .* ' But before we could read any more, the note was whisked away from us again, which I thought was more than a bit suspicious.

I turned to Tallulah, but she was still gazing around the room. 'This room really casts a spell, doesn't it?' she said.

Cyril liked that. 'There isn't a serious book on the supernatural that isn't here. And all these pictures are inspired by real-life sightings of vampires. A few of them were painted by me – including that one.' He pointed to that picture of the hand covered in blood clawing its way out of the ground. 'Vampires believe special powers reside in their hands,' he explained, 'so I wanted to paint a picture of just a vampire hand.

Some experts have pronounced my efforts as outstanding.'

'Maybe he can paint a picture of his ego next,' I whispered to Tallulah, but she didn't smile. Instead, she was gazing at Cyril with such a rapt expression I had to look away – or I'd have thrown up.

Cyril continued, 'You can look in vain for computers in this room, but you won't find any. My uncle and I have no use for them. This shocks you, I expect . . .'

'Well, not actually—' began Tallulah.

'It's all right,' said Cyril. 'My uncle and I know we don't fit into the modern world. That's one thing we have in common with vampires.'

'How do you mean?' I asked.

'Way back in the days of the Greeks and Romans, there were vampires . . .'

'Remember those times, do you?' I murmured.

'Only they weren't monsters then,' said Cyril. 'They belonged to that time when the supernatural was natural. So now you could say they are the last survivors from the days when magic lived. And they are forced to hide in the shadows and keep their identity secret from everyone – or nearly everyone. My uncle has a nose for spotting vampires – a built-in vampire detector, he calls it. Once when I was a boy he let me sit here with him and watch for vampires. And just for a second I caught a glimpse of one floating outside that very window.'

He pointed towards a window which was now pitch-black with just the rain lightly pattering against it.

'Ever since then I've been fascinated by these wild creatures who live alongside humans, yet so secretly they leave little if any trail. They are also completely solitary.'

'But don't they get lonely being on their own all the time?' I asked.

'You must remember,' said Cyril, 'that all vampires share one characteristic. They are creatures with no heart. They care for no one.'

'Cool,' said Tallulah at once.

Surely she didn't really mean that?

Cyril continued, 'Despite all the legends, vampires have caused little harm to humans . . . *until now*.' And there was something very chilling about the slow way he said those last two words.

Cyril moved a little closer to us. Tallulah was gazing at him with such fascination. Why didn't she ever look at me like that? 'Of course, you both know about deadly vampires,' he said, 'as they like to call themselves. They feast on human blood, not because they like it but they believe it contains substances which will give them undreamt-of powers and strength. And that means they, not humans, will rule this earth. And they first surfaced several years ago, right here in Great Walden.'

'I never knew that,' said Tallulah.

'Recent research has discovered more details. Apparently the initial mission didn't last long because they took so much blood from one boy that he died. There was an outcry from the other vampires. Not because the boy was killed, but because such actions threatened their secret identity. Giles, with your help, discovered and humiliated their recent second attempt with a deadly vampire called Elsa Lenchester.'

'We remember,' I muttered.

'Now we are certain they have decided to

restore their honour, which is so vitally important to them, with a third attempt right here. And this time they do not intend to fail. The Blood Ghost is the first manifestation—'

'But,' I interrupted, 'vampires operate at night and this Blood Ghost appeared in the morning.'

'Oh no, no,' cried Cyril excitedly. 'You are talking about the old vampires. Don't forget, these new deadly ones are developing extra powers so they can strike at any time. That woman who was attacked in Calf Lane was just an experiment. Could they attack in the daylight? I'd say it was at least a partial success. There will be many more experiments if we're not careful. And one day soon, we will find there are no limits to these new vampires' powers.' He frowned. 'But I don't even want to think about that. They must be stopped now! That's why we have two missions for you.'

'Great! What are they?' cried Tallulah.

'A warning first,' said Cyril. 'Nothing you do in the rest of your life will be as important as this. But nothing will be as dangerous either.'

CHAPTER FOUR

Thursday 1 January

8.30 p.m. (cont'd)

'In that case,' I said, 'can I go home now?'

'I realize I am asking a lot of you,' said Cyril, 'but I will seek to minimize the danger to you.'

'You don't need to do that,' said Tallulah.

'Yes, you do,' I said.

'Your first mission tonight,' said Cyril, 'is to interview this woman Marilyn, who saw the Blood Ghost. I tried to talk to her earlier but she refused. I think she might be friendlier to two personable young people. And I need to find out something very important from her. Even though she has no memory of it, I am

44

certain the so-called Blood Ghost took blood from her. It planned to take much more but it was interrupted. I need definite proof, though, so I want you to look at her neck.'

'That sounds easy enough,' I said.

'On the right-hand side of her neck,' said Cyril, 'there will be tiny teeth marks hardly visible without a magnifying glass.'

'And we can't go waving one of those in her face,' I said.

'Certainly not,' said Cyril. 'You must be clever and subtle. But if you detect even the smallest mark then we'll have vital proof about the Blood Ghost's true identity. When you find this, text me immediately. I have already prepared your second mission.'

'Which is?' asked Tallulah eagerly.

'To go to the Winter Fair on the common tomorrow evening,' he told her. 'My uncle, who really has a remarkable ability to detect vampires, believes that if a deadly vampire moves in here, that is by far the most likely place it will appear.'

'Why?' I asked.

'Well, it's a perfect location to make a sudden appearance without any questions being asked. Uncle Giles is practically certain that the deadly vampire will be running a stall there as a cover. And so am I.'

'So there will just be one?' I asked.

'There is almost always just one – a kind of trail-blazer first. But if he or she is not stopped – and fast – others will certainly follow.'

'So how are we going to spot this deadly vampire?' I asked.

'It's not easy,' said Cyril. 'But vampires have one distinguishing mark. There are four main types of fingerprints. Vampires have a fifth. It is the one thing they can never disguise. Actually, they don't need to, as only a tiny handful of vampire experts know about this.'

'And you're one of them, of course,' I said.

'Of course.' Then from underneath the table Cyril brought out a huge box of chocolates. 'You, Marcus, bought these for Tallulah.'

'I'm very generous like that,' I said.

'And you will walk all around this winter fair, Tallulah, with this box underneath your arm. Only you must keep dropping the box and asking people to pick it up.'

'Leaving their fingerprints behind as they do so,' said Tallulah.

'Exactly,' said Cyril. 'I want you, Tallulah, to pretend that these chocolates mean a huge amount to you, because they came from your young man. So some real acting might be necessary here.'

Then he smiled. And so did Tallulah. They were having a joke at my expense now. I was disliking Cyril more and more.

'But the important thing is that you keep dropping the box, making it necessary for anyone you even remotely suspect of being a vampire to pick it up. This box is a perfect way of gaining fingerprints. Well, let me demonstrate. One of you touch the box now.'

Immediately I felt nervous. What if half-vampire fingerprints were different too? But Tallulah dived forward and without any hesitation flung her hands down onto the box.

Cyril then brought out talcum powder and dusted the box with it. 'You only need a small amount,' he said. And right away we could see Tallulah's prints. Next Cyril covered the fingerprints with sticky tape and very carefully peeled the tape off – now containing the fingerprints – and placed them on a black card.

'I can tell right away you're not a vampire, Tallulah,' he said. Just for a second I sensed him looking at me, expecting me to take my turn now. So I deliberately turned away and pretended to be staring at a vampire picture on the wall.

'Tomorrow you may well bring me finger-prints of quite a different sort,' he continued.

'Well, let's hope so,' said Tallulah.

Cyril moved forward and all the vampires on the wall seemed to be edging closer to us too. 'Do not take any risks tomorrow, and if you get burned . . .'

'Burned? What do you mean?' I asked.

'Caught in the act somehow,' said Cyril. 'Maybe the deadly vampire works out what you're doing. Do not ever underestimate him – or her. They're very sharp. And if it should challenge you, do not have silly loyalty to me. Give it my name right away. I can deal with it.'

'Can you really?' I asked.

'Of course. Well, I know what I'm dealing with. And I know the vampires' one weakness.'

'So do we,' I said. 'They've got massive egos.' *Like someone else in this room*, I thought.

'It's much more than that. Their pride is overwhelming, and a reflection of their monstrous vanity. That's why, if they are challenged and discovered by what they see as a lowly human, they are so overcome with humiliation that they often decompose on the spot—'

'Been there, done it, got the T-shirt,' I interrupted, a bit rudely. But the way this poseur swaggered about the entire time was really getting up my nose now.

Cyril flinched a bit at my tone. 'Excellent!' he said, then added very smoothly, 'But this time you leave that to me. All you need to do is stay in character – and act like a devoted young couple.' He gave a dry smile. 'Do you think you can do that?'

'We'll practise on the way to Calf Lane,' I said.

'We won't!' cried Tallulah.

'Just remember,' said Cyril, 'there isn't a more dangerous enemy than a deadly vampire. And we are out to sabotage their plans. So the very best of luck, vampire fighters.'

Outside, Tallulah gushed. 'He's totally awesome. I could listen to him for hours.'

'I feel as if I just have.' Then I added, 'Hey, here's an idea: why don't you run back and ask him for an autograph, or better still, a signed photo. Then you can stick it on your wall and gaze lovingly—'

'Even you have to admit he's brave,' Tallulah interrupted.

'Brave! No, I must have missed that.'

'When he said if we're in trouble with the deadly vampire we've to give his name right away.'

'OK, lying back in his weird study he's brave. But just to remind you, we're the ones out tracking down the evil bitey ones.'

'He's planned our whole operation, though – and so brilliantly,' she said.

I had to look away from her then. She'd hardly given me a second glance all evening. Yet it was very risky for me coming here tonight. And if my parents ever found out I'd been with Tallulah – let alone investigating deadly vampires – I would receive the world's greatest rollicking.

Plus I didn't even want to be here. I was doing this solely because of her. And yet all she can do is coo over a creepy poseur who dresses as if he's ninety-six years old. Talk about ungrateful. No wonder I practically hated Tallulah right then.

Actually, I did hate her.

And all that rubbish she spouted about how cool it was for the vampires not to have any heart. Girls are supposed to be more mature than boys. But I'm far, far more mature than Tallulah. So what was I doing hanging around with her? I should just go home now.

'You've gone very quiet,' said Tallulah.

'It's you, you're giving me a headache.'

'How have I done that?' Tallulah actually sounded a bit shocked.

'Having to listen to your voice going on and on about vampires and Cyril . . .'

'Fine. I shan't say another word.'

'That's the best news I've heard all night,' I said.

And we walked in silence the rest of the way to Calf Lane.

CHAPTER FIVE

Thursday 1 January

9.30 p.m.

Calf Lane was incredibly narrow, with no path at all on the side where Marilyn lived. Marilyn's house was a kind of greyish-white colour, with every window hidden behind net curtains. It probably wasn't at all creepy in the day, but now it was.

I'd calmed down a bit by then and I said, 'OK, let's find the vampire's teeth marks and take them outside for questioning.'

Tallulah's lips didn't so much as twitch.

'Don't smile, will you?' I said. 'You might frighten the traffic.'

'I was really looking forward to tonight,'

said Tallulah, 'and you've just spoiled it by acting all moody over nothing.'

'Listen to Little Miss Sunshine,' I said. 'And by the way, one thing I'm not is moody – ask Joel. Ask anyone.'

We were still arguing when the letter box sprang to life. It jumped open so suddenly we both leaped back. It was a bit like someone sticking their tongue out at you. Then a voice hissed out of it, 'What do you want?'

'Oh, hi,' I said, super casually, as if I regularly conversed with letter boxes. 'Sorry to disturb you but we wanted to interview—'

'She's not seeing anyone. She's been talking to people all day and she needs a rest now.'

The letter box snapped shut again, and that seemed to be that until Tallulah shrieked, 'Oh, please help me, I'm doing the interview for the school magazine and I'm in so much trouble at school. I really need this.'

I tell you, Oliver Twist asking for more couldn't have sounded more pitiful. It was a stunning piece of acting, and then we heard another voice – high and shimmery – call out, 'Let the children come in. I can give them a couple of minutes.'

Very grudgingly the door slid open. The man who'd been hissing at us through the letter box muttered, 'Wipe your feet and follow me.' He led us into a sitting room crammed with plants and photos, every one of which featured the lady who was reclining on a massive couch.

She was dressed up as if she were off to a ball. But she was lying very still and at first I thought she was asleep. But two bright alert eyes peered up at me and then she patted her hair, which was red and stretched down past her shoulders. She kept stroking this hair just as if it were a little pet beside her.

And then . . . well, neither Tallulah nor I could help it: we both started gawping intently at her neck. For here lurked the absolutely vital clue. But there was only one light on in this room, and it was hard to see Marilyn that clearly – let alone her neck.

'It's all right, I don't bite, you know,' said Marilyn. That made me want to laugh – a lot.

Then Tallulah, still gazing hard at Marilyn's neck, said, 'This is so kind of you.'

Marilyn nodded in agreement. Then she pointed at the figure hovering behind us. 'My husband isn't normally such a grump, but people just won't stop asking me questions today and he worries about me.'

'But you're big news,' I said.

'Yes, I suppose I am,' she agreed. 'Well, sit down for a moment.'

'She can't give you long, though,' muttered her husband.

'We realize that,' said Tallulah, getting out her notebook, while still sneaking glances at Marilyn's neck. 'If you could just tell us what you saw.'

'Oh, I'll remember it until the day I die,' said Marilyn. 'That figure just stepping up out of the darkness.' And then she didn't so much tell us as recite once more her meeting with the Blood Ghost.

Finally she added, 'Worst of all, I sensed this figure meant me great harm and I was in the biggest danger of my whole life.' She gave a little laugh. 'Of course that sounds so absurd now. What could this ghost – this lost, dead person, as the ghost expert called it – do to me?'

But she hadn't met a dead person. She'd been attacked by one of the undead. And I was sure its teeth marks were there on her too. If only I could identify them for certain.

I glanced at Tallulah questioningly. She shook her head. So she hadn't spotted them either. Then Marilyn's husband charged back in with a mobile phone. 'Did you say you'd answer questions on a radio phone-in?'

'I believe I did.'

'Well,' he said, 'they want to talk to you down the line in one minute.'

'It never stops,' said Marilyn. 'But I hope you've got some good material for your school magazine.'

We couldn't hang around any longer. But we still didn't have any definite proof. That's why I sprang forward and said, 'You've been so great, may I give you a hug?'

Marilyn looked startled but pleased. She stretched out her arms. Soon I was engulfed by her red hair and a mighty whiff of lavender. But there they were, on the right side of her neck, just as Cyril had said: tiny teeth marks.

And for a moment something else seemed to have slipped into the room with us. Something cunning and savage and cruel, and totally heartless.

And Marilyn was saying, 'I just wish I didn't feel so tired all the time. I hardly have the energy to get off this couch and that's not like me. Everyone says it's delayed shock . . .'

But I knew it was nothing to do with delayed shock. She'd been the victim of a deadly vampire taking blood from her. And if it hadn't been interrupted it would have taken more, wiping out all her memories, wiping out Marilyn herself – and for what? So the deadly vampires could gain more power, more dark magic.

Up till now I really couldn't have cared less about deadly vampires. I was only here because I liked a girl . . . nothing else. But all at once I was so choked up with anger, I was practically shaking. And even when I spoke to Tallulah outside I was still seething. 'That deadly vampire – it's got to be stopped,' I said.

Tallulah gave me one of her piercing stares

and said quietly, 'Don't worry, we'll get it – and fast – we're a good team.'

I stared at her. 'You didn't just pay me a compliment, did you?'

'Me? Never,' she said, smiling faintly.

All the bad feeling from earlier seemed to have just melted away. Why was I bothered about Cyril anyway? We'd only have to see him once more to give him the chocolates back. Then he'd pose off, while Tallulah and I – we were a good team.

I was so chuffed with her saying that, I laughed at myself. And it never entered my head not to continue with this mission now. So we arranged to meet at the fair at seven o'clock tomorrow, to catch the deadly vampire.

But first I've got to go home – and do those stupid relaxation exercises with my mum and dad.

CHAPTER SIX

Thursday 1 January

10.30 p.m.

'We're in the sitting room,' trilled Mum as I opened the front door. 'All ready for you.'

And so they were, both lying on the carpet and waving their hands in the air. 'We've been doing some hand relaxation exercises first,' announced Mum.

'Of course you have,' I murmured.

'Well, come and join us,' said Mum.

'First I think I'll just take a picture,' I said. 'I'll call it a typical night at home with my parents.'

Mum stopped twitching her hands. 'No, you can't do that.'

'Oh, shame.'

'Now, come on,' said Dad. 'Lie on the floor and we'll all chant together.'

'Hey, rather than waste all that oxygen, why don't I just chant very quietly upstairs?'

'No, we're doing this as a family,' snapped Mum.

'Fine, fine, let's all be weirdos together.' I shot down onto the carpet and promptly got the giggles. And then Dad, to his huge embarrassment, started laughing too. Soon both he and I were rolling around the floor laughing our heads off.

'You're as bad as him,' said Mum, jumping up.

'I'm sorry,' gasped Dad.

'And we are relaxing,' I spluttered.

Mum didn't answer, but later she'd calmed down a bit. And I've promised her faithfully that I'll fall asleep chanting *I'm a really great half-vampire*', and it'll be the first thing I say tomorrow as well.

Friday 2 January

6.45 a.m.

Only when I woke up I never got a chance to say any of that 'Hey, I'm a really great half-vampire' stuff – because something was in my bedroom.

I could hear it fluttering about behind my curtains. What on earth was it? A small bird, perhaps – or a bat? I didn't have a clue. But it kept on beating and flapping against the curtains, desperate to escape. And any moment I knew it would. That's when every part of me shuddered with total horror.

I really didn't want to see what came out from behind those curtains as I knew it meant me harm. But I couldn't move either. So I just lay there, frozen with terror – until I woke up.

I was gasping with relief then. So I'd still been dreaming, when I thought I was awake. But it was all over now. I knew that, but I just hated seeing my curtains closed. I kept on imagining something very sinister was still lurking behind there.

I knew it was stupid, but it was all I could think about. So finally I tore out of bed, and with one heave pulled the curtains right back.

Nothing there, of course.

Only there was something floating right outside my window.

A hand.

A skeletal hand dripping with blood.

CHAPTER SEVEN

Friday 2 January

6.45 a.m. (cont'd)

The hand wriggled and twisted. And before I knew it, a second hand was there.

It too was covered in blood and writhed about madly. I could just about make out a shape behind the hands as well. But it was very misty and unclear. All I could really see was those hands. It was as if they were trying to send me a message. And I had to know what it was. I found myself moving even closer until my face was right up against the glass.

That's when the message crept into my head: '*Let me in. You must let me in.*'

Now I absolutely knew I mustn't do that. I

had to turn away now. But somehow I couldn't. My eyes were positively glued to those dancing hands. *'Let me in. You must let me in.'*

I even started to pull at the handle. I mean, how crazy was that? The figure outside my window was stalking me. I was its prey. Yet I was helping it inside because . . . because those hands were hypnotizing me, locking me into its deadly vampire power.

I knew this, but still I went on unbolting the window. Any moment now I'd let it in.

Then in a terrifying flash I saw what would happen next. It would instantly transform into a deadly vampire bat and lunge straight for my throat. So I had to stop now. The only way I could do that was to look right away from it. Do you know, that was the toughest thing I've ever done. I had to really, really concentrate.

But I did it.

After which I closed my eyes tightly. So there was no chance of those skeleton hands casting a spell on me again. Only now I couldn't see a thing. Still, I was in my bedroom – a place I knew exceedingly well – so I rocketed back to where I thought my bed was. Only I totally missed and smashed into my bedside table instead, sending bottles and hairbrushes cannoning everywhere. What a racket. I was sure my parents would come tumbling in. But amazingly they slept through it all.

So I crouched by the bedside table with my eyes still firmly shut. Finally I stood up slowly, opened my eyes, peered around and allowed myself one quick glance outside. No blood-soaked hands lurking there now. I'd won that round, I suppose.

But I didn't feel an atom of triumph. I was too dazed and shocked and scared. For I had been visited by the Blood Ghost. Why?

Was I like Marilyn – just an unlucky victim? Or had it come searching especially for me? Maybe it knew I'd visited Marilyn last night and was on its trail?

And was it now warning me off? Was it saying, *I know where you live and if you don't stay out of this I'll be back?*

7.20 a.m.

If it wanted to scare me, it's succeeded all right. I'm still shaking now. So it's won. Only it sort of hasn't. You see, I hate being told what to do by anyone. It doesn't matter if it's teachers, parents – or blood ghosts. So there's a part of me now that wants to track down the deadly vampire even more keenly than I did before.

Hey, I sound almost brave, don't I? Well, it won't last, I can promise you that. But I so want that feeling to stay until tonight when Tallulah and I get those fingerprints. That's all I've got to do, dead simple really, and then it's over to mighty poseur.

But I'll have played a part in stopping that deadly vampire.

That'll teach it to peek through my window.

7.35 a.m.

While I'm feeling so unnaturally brave I've come to another decision. I'm going to ask Tallulah out at the fair tonight. Last night she said we were a good team. And Tallulah hardly ever says stuff like that. So it was a massive deal. Was she even hinting we should go out together? Maybe. Anyway, time to stop dithering and do something.

Hey, if I can face the Blood Ghost first thing this morning, surely I can ask a girl out.

7.36 a.m.

Yeah, even Tallulah.

7.37 a.m.

Plus, if we do find this deadly vampire tonight, Tallulah will be overjoyed, so there'll probably never be a better moment.

9.30 a.m.

I went down to breakfast even though I wasn't at all hungry. My stomach still felt all knotted up.

'So, how are you?' asked Mum, switching on her full-beam smile. 'Any tingles in your hands at all?'

'No tingles at all,' I said flatly, still wondering if I could get away without eating anything.

'Never mind,' said Mum. 'Now, what did you promise you'd keep saying over and over?'

But I was hardly listening to her. The Blood Ghost's early-morning call had wiped everything else from my brain cells. So I just looked blank.

Mum's voice rose. *'Hey, I'm a really great half-vampire, so happy with everything.* Now go on, you say it.'

I shouldn't have tried to be funny here, but I did and said, 'Hey, Mum's a really great half-vampire, so happy with everything.'

No smiles! Instead, Dad took a large gulp of tea while Mum went all tight-lipped.

'Why are you always working against us?' she hissed at last.

'I'm not,' I said. 'Over Christmas – yes, the Christmas holidays – I went to that crammer and tried my best. And if you'd stop pressurizing me every minute of the day, then the special power might just happen naturally – or it might not. But you nagging me every single second doesn't help at all. It just—'

'That's enough,' interrupted Dad quietly.

Mum got up and started noisily slamming plates into the dishwasher.

Dad stared at her, and then at me. 'We've just got to keep positive,' he said to no one in particular.

6.35 p.m.

First, I went to Joel's house tonight, to check my alibi (my parents think I'm helping Joel again). He was waiting for me at the door.

'Your mum's only gone and told my parents I'm having problems with Katie. So now they've given me this.' He flung a leaflet at me which said: UNDERSTANDING YOUR EMOTIONS – A GUIDE FOR TEENAGE BOYS.

'Lots of good reading there,' I said.

'Plus I've had to listen to my dad giving me all this advice about relationships, his face bright red the whole time he was talking. I'm scarred for life now.'

'I owe you big time for this,' I said.

'You really do. So, how are you getting on with Dracula's daughter?'

'Things are progressing,' I said.

'Have you kissed her yet?'

'Maybe.'

'That means no. You're probably not even holding hands.'

'Well, I am asking her out tonight,' I announced.

Joel stepped back from me. 'You, sir, are a very brave man.'

'I know.'

7.20 p.m.

Tallulah actually arrived late at the Winter

Fair. I was a bit peeved about this, but then I saw she was out of breath.

'Very sorry,' she gasped. This was highly unusual. Tallulah never apologized. 'But I couldn't get out.'

'Why not?'

'I'm being watched practically every second.'

She made it sound as if she'd just broken out of some high-security prison. 'Who's watching you? Your parents?'

'Yeah, they keep saying how I've got to . . .' But then she waved her hand dismissively, as if brushing them away. 'They'd never understand how I couldn't miss tonight.'

'Seeing me, you mean. Well, I'm very flattered.'

She just ignored this. 'I texted Cyril that we'd seen the vampire marks on Marilyn's neck.'

'Well, actually, it was only me who saw them, but I'll let you steal some of the glory. So how many gold stars did Cyril text you, then?'

'Oh, millions, I couldn't count them all.'

Tallulah was actually making little jokes. Incredible. She seemed very worked up too, though. And I didn't understand why her family were keeping her under constant surveillance. Had she done something really bad over Christmas? Or was she still ill? Yes, that must be it.

I was about to ask her when she said, 'Cyril left a message for you.'

'Oh, yeah?'

'He said to tell you not to eat any of the chocolates in the box as they've been in there quite a while.'

I could hear Cyril saying that too, and laughing in a patronizing way about me with Tallulah. The sooner he vanished off the scene the better.

'So what have you been up to?' asked Tallulah.

If I told her about my early-morning visitor she'd go on and on about it – and probably contact Cyril. Besides, I'd finally stopped shivering inside. Anyway, the very last thing I wanted was to start talking about it again. So I just shrugged and said, 'Oh, nothing much.'

There was a long queue into the Winter Fair and this man bounced about trying to entertain the crowd. He was dressed up as a snowman, wearing a white fluffy coat with black buttons, a large black hat, a scarf and big black boots. He'd painted his face white and had also stuck on a fake red nose. And he was laughing so loudly he made Father Christmas seem positively gloomy.

He bounded over to us and glanced at me. And just for a second a look of recognition, followed by what I can only call sheer hatred, passed across his face. It was very swift. Tallulah didn't even notice it. But I did.

So he knew I was a half-vampire. Vampires can often spot us right away. They don't like us either (the feeling is mutual) but this was more than that − the burning hatred that sneaked out of his eyes for a second.

What did I do to cause that? Nothing, unless he was the Blood Ghost who'd visited me this morning. Unless he thought he'd warned me off. Yet here I was, defying him and on his trail. I felt proud of myself and very scared, both at once.

But the snowman quickly recovered and ran through his usual patter again. 'Welcome, you two, to the greatest Winter Fair ever.' That smile was as wide as ever now, but it never reached his eyes. They were lifeless. No one was ever at home behind them.

I whispered to Tallulah, 'Drop the box now.' She gave me a surprised look, but let the box slip out of her hand.

'Look at that,' chortled the snowman. 'Throwing your gift away already. Still, that's girls for you.'

We both waited for him to pick up the box. At last he did, with a great flourish and a panoramic view of his yellow teeth. 'Well, here you are, young lady, and I won't even ask you to offer me a chocolate.' Then he gave a laugh that was so deafening it made my eardrums ring as he went thumping off down the queue.

'Do you really think he . . . ?' began Tallulah.

'Yeah, I do,' I said.

I felt certain we'd met the Blood Ghost already.

CHAPTER EIGHT

Friday 2 January

7.55 p.m.

Tallulah is now charging around the fair finger-printing just about everyone with fingers.

First of all she decided the grubby-looking guy who stamped our hands after we'd paid our entrance fee looked 'dead suspicious' (to me he just looked dead miserable), so she dropped her box of chocolates in front of him before getting out a small notebook in which she was jotting down a brief description of everyone whose prints she'd taken – and exactly where they were on the chocolate box. He rather grudgingly picked it up and she grinned triumphantly at me.

Then she was off trailing her next suspect – a middle-aged guy in the most obnoxiously bright shirt I'd ever seen. He was taking money for the dodgem cars.

'No vampire would be seen dead in a shirt like that,' I said.

Then she was off again, until I hissed, 'You're dropping that box about three times a minute and people are going to start noticing you. You've got to ease off a bit.'

Tallulah eased off and just contented herself with staring very keenly at everyone working at a stall. The fair itself was a blaze of lights, thumping music and piercing 'Ooohs' from the people on the big wheel as it swung high in the air.

'Any one of these people here,' said Tallulah, 'could suffer at the hands of the deadly vampire if we don't find him or her first. We're really here on a very important mission.'

'I guess we are, although I still say *he's* suspect number one.' I nodded at the snowman. I watched him roaming around the fair now, shaking hands with some little kids and nearly falling over with laughter at something he'd said to them. (They weren't laughing at all.)

'You just don't like him,' said Tallulah.

But it was much, much more than that.

8.15 p.m.

You really won't believe this. I can't believe it myself. But we've lost the box of chocolates.

We'd gone over to Zena's shooting gallery. The woman in charge seemed to have just one giant tooth, which she whistled through every time she spoke.

'Now, she looks like the most harmless person in the world,' I said. 'So we must definitely check her out.'

As we drew near Zena immediately thrust a gun at me, saying, 'Come on, win one of our lovely prizes for your young lady.'

'Oh yes, do win me something,' cooed Tallulah. She really was a far better actress than I'd ever imagined. But the prizes themselves looked very cheap – tiny teddies and indignant-looking dolls.

Still, I wanted to win something for 'my girl', so I took care aiming, while noticing out of the corner of my eye Tallulah putting her chocolates down. Then she seemed to forget about them and stood watching me very intently.

My first two shots just missed. 'So close, dear,' said Zena. 'Try again.'

And my third and final shot did hit something. Zena looked surprised and a bit cross. But she presented the smallest and most weather-beaten teddy I'd ever seen to Tallulah, who clapped her hands in delight.

We walked off slowly together, expecting Zena to call out that we'd left the chocolates behind. We moved on a bit further, but Zena still didn't say anything.

'We'll have to go back,' said Tallulah.

By the time we'd returned to her stall, trade had picked up. There was even a small queue. Then Zena spotted us. 'Come for another go, have you?' she said, but she didn't seem anywhere near as friendly as before.

'No, it's just I left some chocolates behind,' said Tallulah.

'I didn't notice,' said Zena briskly.

We showed her where Tallulah had placed the chocolates. Only they weren't there now. We both stood rooted to the spot for a moment with shock and horror.

'You probably left them somewhere else,' said Zena.

'No, I know they were here,' said Tallulah. But Zena had already waddled away.

We both peered at the spot where Tallulah had left the chocolates, as if they were going to suddenly spring up out of a trap door. But no such luck.

'She's taken them,' said Tallulah, 'because she knows what we're up to and is the deadly vampire.'

'Or someone else who's the deadly vampire – like the snowman – guessed what we were doing and followed us,' I said. 'And the moment we put the chocolates down he grabbed them.'

At that very moment the snowman came rolling past us.

'I bet he's hidden them somewhere,' I said. 'Or alternatively,' I added, 'they could have just been nicked by someone who likes chocolates – well, they're about to get a very nasty surprise, aren't they?'

Tallulah didn't answer: she just murmured, 'We'll have to split up and search the entire fair. Let's meet back here in fifteen minutes.'

Well, I've raced about and found nothing.

And now, here's Tallulah coming over to me and not looking at all happy either. More soon.

8.50 p.m.

What a truly bizarre half-hour. We found the chocolates all right, only we haven't got them now because . . . but I'm jumping ahead.

Let's go back to the moment when Tallulah came storming towards me shouting, 'Where are those chocolates? Where are they? Why can't we find them?'

'OK, just calm down.'

'Don't you dare tell me to calm down,' cried Tallulah. 'I despise people who say that to me.' She added, 'I think we should return to the scene of the crime.'

'Good idea,' I agreed.

So we steamed back to Zena's stall, now doing a roaring trade, with guns exploding all over the place. I glanced idly at all the so-called special prizes for those lucky people who hit three bull's-eyes in a row. There was a maggoty-looking doll and . . . that's when I jumped into the air like a demented salmon.

'Our chocolates . . .' I began.

'What about them?'

'Look!' I pointed, and then she saw them too.

'Zena's stolen our chocolates,' she shrieked, 'and now she's trying to pass them off as a big prize.'

'Well, let's face it, the chocs give her shoddy prizes a touch of much-needed class.'

'But she's not going to get away with it,' cried Tallulah.

Without another word we marched up to Zena, who looked distinctly unexcited to see us again. 'Excuse me, but can we have our chocolates back, please?' I said.

'The chocolates you stole from us,' said Tallulah.

'I don't know what you're talking about,' said Zena, turning to another customer.

'Oh, yes you do,' said Tallulah, her voice rising. 'I put those chocolates down for a moment and when I came back for them you pretended you didn't know where they were, when actually you'd nicked them from us. And if you think I'm talking loudly now, you should hear me when I start yelling.'

'You really don't want to hear that,' I said. 'And by the way, I can shout too, and here's a quick demonstration.' I put back my head and yelled, 'All prizes on this stall are rubbish – apart from the one she stole from us.' Then, in a normal voice I said, 'Already we've got people's attention.' And we had. 'So you just wait until my friend here starts. I tell you, banshees go to her for tips.'

Zena scowled at Tallulah and me. 'Pair of tricksters, that's what you are.'

'*We're* tricksters!' cried Tallulah.

Zena grabbed the chocolates from the super prizes display and hurled them at Tallulah. 'I hope they choke you,' she snapped.

'And a Very Unhappy New Year to you too,' I said.

We dashed away, grinning. 'No one messes with us,' I said triumphantly.

But Tallulah was peering anxiously at the chocolates. 'We need to check none of the fingerprints have been rubbed off.' We stopped in front of the Big Wheel while she peered at the chocolates with a magnifying glass and checked her small notebook.

'No, they're all here,' she said at last. 'Zena

obviously just nicked them to improve her prize collection.'

Before I could reply, a familiar voice – Cyril's – hissed from behind us, 'Whatever you do, don't turn round. Just nod your head if you've managed to get the fingerprints of the man dressed up as a snowman.'

Tallulah nodded her head while I asked Cyril, 'Do you think he's the person we're looking for, then?'

'I strongly suspect he's the vilest example of that species I've ever seen,' whispered Cyril, 'and is highly dangerous. But his fingerprints will be the clinching proof. I need those before I can swing into action. But it's too dangerous for you to be seen talking to me. My uncle and I are not unknown to vampires and I fear that the snowman may well have recognized me. So would you, Tallulah, step back and, as quickly and un-self-consciously as possible, slip the chocolates into my bag which I am now holding open?'

Tallulah did that in a flash, dropping in her notebook too so that Cyril would know whose fingerprints were whose.

'Deftly done,' hissed Cyril approvingly. 'I

need to immediately check if my instincts are correct. So I shall leave this fair now. Please hang around here a little longer acting naturally and do not contact me again. I feel bad involving you at all. But you should be extremely proud of yourselves. It's time for me to step up to the mark now. I will text you my findings. Good night.' And with that he strode away.

'Well, I wasn't expecting that,' I said. 'Still, it looks like we've found him.'

'Yes,' agreed Tallulah, but she looked totally deflated. I knew it had all finished too abruptly for her. 'I expect Cyril will let us know if the snowman really is . . . who we think he is,' she said.

'Bound to. Well, you anyway. You're teacher's pet.'

She looked at me. 'But you guessed the snowman's true identity right away. How?'

'Let's just call me a genius and leave it at that.'

'Well, our work here is done,' said Tallulah.

'Cyril said we should hang around for a bit, though,' I said. And I didn't want her sloping off home, especially when I still had a really important question to ask her. I needed to pick the right moment for that. And this certainly wasn't it. Then I spotted over the entrance to a tent a sign that said: CONSULT THE WORLD'S ONLY VENTRILOQUIST FORTUNE-TELLER.

'That might be a laugh,' I said.

Tallulah shook her head. 'I just think fortune-tellers are stupid – and ventriloquists too.'

'So, double stupid. Excellent – come on.'

A morose-looking boy hovered outside selling tickets. 'Four pounds for two,' he chanted at us.

'Money back if it doesn't come true?' I asked.

The boy frowned and said again, 'Four pounds for two.'

Inside, the tent was very cramped and dimly lit. We could just make out two chairs in front of a small table. Then we heard a high, child-like voice from the end of the tent say, 'Sit down, make yourself at home.'

'Thanks, we will,' I said.

The speaker's lips were turned down at the corners as if he'd just tasted something really disagreeable. His cheeks and lips were painted bright red. And his eyes were wide and staring.

I'd been chatting with a ventriloquist's dummy.

Then from out of the shadows loomed the ventriloquist. He had horn-rimmed glasses and a neat moustache and was wearing an old crumpled suit. He also had gloves on and smelled of very strong aftershave. He was hunched over the dummy, which was perched on his lap. 'Welcome. My name is Mr Rathbone, and you've already met Hugo, my assistant.' His voice was totally different to Hugo's – low and very polite.

'Assistant? What are you talking about? I'm the brains of this outfit.'

'Quiet, Hugo,' said Mr Rathbone. 'Have no fear, you are dealing with an expert fortune-teller.'

'That's me, of course,' said Hugo in his weird, high-pitched voice.

'Well, I can see you're no dummy,' I said.

Hugo gave an odd chuckle.

We sat down and Tallulah asked, 'Are you going to start shuffling cards now?' She sounded surprisingly anxious.

'We don't need cards. It's your hands which tell your real future,' said Mr Rathbone. At that moment a lamp came on right where Tallulah and I were sitting.

'Now place your hands . . .' began Mr Rathbone.

'Oh, let me say it, please,' said Hugo.

It really did seem as if two different people were talking.

'Well, say it very clearly,' said Mr Rathbone.

'Place your hands, palm upwards, on the table under the light,' said Hugo. 'Now, who's going first?'

'You,' said Tallulah firmly to me.

'You won't see a better hand than this one,' I said cheerily, but for some reason my heart was beating furiously.

'What's your name?' asked Hugo.

'Pat – Pat Peanuts.' Don't ask me why but I didn't want to give them my real name.

'Well, Pat, hold your hand still and let us concentrate,' said Hugo.

There was silence for a moment, then he

let out a strange, grisly snarl which made both Tallulah and me jump. It was like a cross between a growl and a very loud burp.

'Hey, my hand isn't as bad as that, is it?' I asked.

'I'm sorry about that,' said Mr Rathbone. 'Hugo gets a bit over-excited sometimes and makes these ridiculous noises. Apologize, Hugo.'

'I'm sorry,' said Hugo quickly, 'but you've got such an unusual hand, Pat. In fact, I've never seen a hand like it.'

'Sheer quality there,' I said.

'Your life-line just goes on and on,' went on Hugo. 'The only thing is' – his voice suddenly grew lower – 'there's a break in your life-line.'

'Which is nothing to worry about,' cut in Mr Rathbone.

'Oh, yes it is,' said Hugo. 'A break in your life-line means great danger. And this break is quite soon, very soon, in fact. So you must take great care over the next few days and don't – don't take unnecessary risks. Keep out of things which might be dangerous. It's very important to remember that.'

'Hey, you're starting to make my skin crawl now,' I said, taking my hand away. 'I think I'll stop there.'

'Better be safe than sorry,' said Hugo, and then he added, 'By the way, we're never wrong. Now, what is your name?' He turned to Tallulah.

'Margot,' said Tallulah. So she was giving a false name too. I stifled a giggle.

'Well, hold your hands out, Margot, palms upward, nice and slowly,' said Hugo.

Tallulah's hands began to edge forward very slowly. But then they sprang back again as if she'd just been bitten. She leaped to her feet. 'No time. We've got to go.'

And with that she just fled.

I stared after her in amazement and then jumped up too. 'I won't say I've had a good time, because I haven't. But thanks for – well, something.'

'Sorry if we upset anyone,' said Hugo.

'You always go too far, Hugo,' said Mr Rathbone. 'In future, I will do all the fortune-telling.'

I left them bickering away and charged out of the tent and over to Tallulah. She was turned away from me. She wasn't crying, was she?

'Tallulah?' I said.

She sprang round and practically shouted, 'That act was clearly phoney. So why waste my time on it?' She laughed jerkily.

I touched her lightly on the shoulder. 'Are you sure you're OK?'

'Why wouldn't I be?' She laughed again. 'But it was just such rubbish, and I didn't like him saying all that stuff about you being in danger.'

'I wasn't so keen on that either.'

'Oh, he'd probably have seen even worse things in my hand,' she said.

I looked at her sharply. 'How do you mean?'

But Tallulah ignored this question and announced, 'I'm off to the loo, but when I come back we've got to go *there*.'

I saw where she was pointing and grinned.

Any moment now she'll be back and that's when I shall ask her out. Well, we've the perfect setting, which she picked out herself – the ghost train.

CHAPTER NINE

Friday 2 January

9.15 p.m.

Yeah, I've done it.

I've finally asked Tallulah out.

She and I found a carriage to ourselves on the ghost train. And soon it was swaying away through this dark tunnel. Coffins started opening with skeletons popping out – which were about as frightening as fluffy white kittens. And I said, 'Actually, Tallulah, there's something I want to talk to you about.'

She leaned forward enthusiastically. 'Is it about that ventriloquist? Because I've been thinking about him too.'

'No, no, it's nothing to do with him. So

will you just listen for a minute and hear me out?'

I paused to let the rotting head of a corpse whizz past us. I've seen scarier-looking apples. Then I took the deepest breath of my life and said, 'I've been thinking about you a lot because I really like you. So this brings me round to asking if you'd like to be my friend who's a girl, otherwise known as a girlfriend. And that's it really, except to say that a big yes right now would be mind-blowingly brilliant.'

And then the whole world stopped. I'm sure it did. It was as if a giant pause button had been hit, and all I could hear was my heart booming so fast I thought there was a strong possibility I could explode right then in that ghost train.

But then the world started up again and Tallulah was shaking her head at me. 'What did you say that for? You've spoiled everything now by being stupid.'

She was royally annoyed with me. But why exactly? And what did she mean I'd spoiled everything? I didn't get it. Hadn't I just paid her a massive compliment? A vampire in a big swishy cape started flapping about like a mad crow. Normally Tallulah and I would have killed ourselves laughing at it. But we hardly noticed it. Instead, we were both staring miserably at nothing in particular.

'I don't know what I've done wrong,' I said at last.

'Look, I just haven't got the time for this,' Tallulah hissed back at me.

'I'm very sorry for ruining your schedule.' Then something unseen brushed against our cheeks with a blood-curdling squeak and the ghost train came creaking to a halt.

Tallulah was scrambling to get out before it had even stopped. This guy in charge of the ghost train said to her, 'Just wait a second, love.' But she didn't listen and sped away. He shook his head at me. 'Something must have really scared her.'

'Yeah, it did. Me,' I muttered.

I didn't rush to try and catch her up.

In the few minutes we'd been on the ghost train the weather seemed to have turned much heavier and darker with rain splattering down too. I was convinced Tallulah would be long gone, but actually she was waiting for me.

Looking very grave, she said, 'What you just said in there, it never happened – all right?'

She was acting as if I'd said something utterly disgusting to her. Actually she was really irritating me now. But I said, 'I apologize for getting mushy and uncool. It will never happen with you again.'

She actually flinched then, before saying quickly, 'Never mind that, I've got something very important to tell you.'

'Just tell me it's not about vampires.'

'Well, it is, actually.'

'I might have known it.'

'And stop shouting that word out. You don't know who is listening. Anyway, Cyril's just texted me. The fingerprints of the snowman proved positive.' She waved her phone at me.

'Great, so that's it, our part in this is over,' I said.

'No, it isn't, as I think there's more than one of them here.'

'Your precious Cyril said vampires are solitary and—'

'I know that, but in this case it's different. I believe the ventriloquist is a V person too.'

93

'Is that why you ran out?'

'No, not exactly. But I've been thinking about it since. That whole set-up was so odd. And he was wearing gloves.'

'Oh wow, arrest him now.'

'But it meant he would never give his fingerprints away. And then what he was saying to you about being in danger soon. No real fortune-teller would blurt it out like that. He knew we were on to him and was telling us to stay away. So we both ought to go and see Cyril right now and tell him my theory.'

I didn't move. I just looked at her for a long moment, and then said quietly, 'I'd rather roast my own eyeballs.'

Tallulah stared at me, not believing what I was saying. I savoured her shock. It made up a little bit for all the hurt and bewilderment and disappointment she'd caused me on the ghost train.

I went on, 'I've just resigned from being a vampire fighter. So it'll be just you and Cyril having a nice, cosy chat together. Still, that won't bother you, will it?'

Tallulah hadn't seen that coming at all.

But then she recovered and shouted, 'Right, fine, I don't need you.'

'Owned,' I shouted back. 'That's exactly how I feel.' And that was the very last thing I said to her before she stormed away.

9.35 p.m.

I sloped around the fair for a bit, but not visiting any of the so-called attractions. My own thoughts were keeping me too busy. I did pause outside the ventriloquist's tent. I hadn't liked it in there any more than Tallulah. But I didn't like it inside the headmaster's office either, and that didn't make him a vampire.

10.15 p.m.

I'm still not home – because I met someone on the way.

The Blood Ghost.

CHAPTER TEN

Friday 2 January

10.30 p.m.

I thought I'd had my fill of the Blood Ghost – at least for today.

But I've obviously been prescribed a double dose of terror.

I'd just charged through Brent Woods. The rain was bucketing down now and the sky seemed to be getting darker every second. So I was massively relieved to get out of there.

But then the sky seemed to split apart. There were giant hailstones everywhere and it felt as if millions of arrows were being fired into my face all at once.

The only good thing about hailstones is

that they never last too long. So I took shelter under a clump of trees, angry with myself for staying out for so long. I could have been safely at home now, instead of just drooping about the fair. But I couldn't get the way Tallulah had acted out of my head – not even now, with zillions of hailstones beating away at me.

At last they started to subside. But that's when I heard an urgent high-pitched screech, like a mad bird shrieking – the very sound Marilyn had heard just before the Blood Ghost had materialized. It was eerie and unearthly and yet – and this was very odd – I felt as if I recognized that voice somehow.

Still, this wasn't the time to think about that. I knew I only had a moment to run away fast. But then, like smoke, the Blood Ghost just moved beside me, its blood-covered hands twisting and wriggling again. I was so shocked, but I desperately tried to keep my wits about me. I knew I must look away from it this time. And I was still backing away when it vanished – just as suddenly as it had appeared.

'Only a quick show tonight, then,' I said,

shaking with relief – until something dropped
out of the sky at me.

The Blood Ghost had, in the blink of an
eye, transformed into a vampire's more trad-
itional form – a bat. Only this blazing streak
of fury came at me with such force I nearly
fell over. But I couldn't do that, as the moment
it landed even the smallest bite on my neck
it'd be all over. I'd be unconscious in seconds.
Already I was fighting to catch my breath.

Somehow I had to stay on my feet and fight
it off. I pulled my jersey up over one half of
my neck (if only I'd worn a scarf) and started
beating it off with my other hand.

The bat hurtled straight at the exposed
part of my neck. I could feel its wings whirling
against my face. It was getting closer. If only
someone else was here to help. But no one
seemed to be about.

While my breathing was getting more and
more ragged, the bat hissed and snapped
impatiently. And its eyes blazed furiously.

Was it the snowman? It had to be.

Only I wasn't just being warned off this
time – I was being wiped out. And one small
bite on my neck was all it would take. But

the snowman wasn't going to win. I even felt a tiny bit confident that I could see off this monster.

Until, right before my eyes, the bat began to grow. Suddenly it was twice as large as before. And now it seemed to fill the whole sky with its dark menace as it leaped exultantly at me.

The shock and horror of that just overwhelmed me. All at once I lost my balance and went toppling onto the ground.

Nothing could save me now.

CHAPTER ELEVEN

Friday 2 January

10.45 p.m.

As I lay there I saw a flash of very sharp teeth and a tremor shivered all the way down my spine. Any second, I thought, those teeth would be biting into my neck and I'd become its very own private blood bank. What a lousy end to a truly lousy night.

The bat let out another screech. It absolutely stank too. And if I hadn't been so terrified I'd have thrown up. But instead, I somehow began staggering to my feet like a boxer who had almost, but not quite, been knocked out of a fight.

I gazed blearily at it. I started to hunch my

shoulders up and raise my fists. But it was too late. I felt it starting to sink its teeth into me.

In a wild frenzy I swung out and pulled it off. But it dived right back at me. This was hopeless. It was only a matter of time before it dealt me the fatal blow.

And then I heard – or thought I heard – footsteps pounding towards me. Was I dreaming this before I passed out? I felt so weak and groggy now. But the sound grew even louder. Who could it be? Tallulah? Cyril? But instead a voice I'd never heard in my life before yelled, 'Get off him!'

A boy in a big raincoat was valiantly and brilliantly trying to pull this giant bat off me. It immediately flew at him with another ear-splitting screech. The boy clamped one hand over his face while trying to fight it off with the other.

Watching him seemed to send fresh energy flowing through me, which was just as well as the bat had sent the boy reeling back and swooped down onto me again. It began tearing madly at me.

I reached out and pulled both my arms up

and around the bat's neck, and somehow sent it rocketing right away from me.

'Hey, that was brilliant,' called the boy who'd got up and was standing right beside me now. 'Don't worry, we'll get it next time.'

I nodded, but my last effort had nearly wiped me out. I crouched over, struggling to breathe while waiting for the bat to reappear. We were both tensing up, ready. But it never did. It had vanished into the dark sky as swiftly as a bad dream.

'Did all that just happen?' said the boy at last.

But I still wasn't able to breathe properly, let alone talk, while the boy couldn't, it seemed, stop talking. 'I'd heard of seagulls going mad – well, a boy in my class accidentally disturbed their nest and they just went for him. He said they were just incredibly scary. But that bat was something else – and so massive. What has it got against you, anyway?'

'Funny, I forgot to ask it,' I said.

The boy grinned then. He was about my age, but bigger, with a mop of curly hair and a large, cheeky face. It was strange I'd never noticed him around the village before. As if reading my mind he said, 'I haven't lived here long. And then I caught the flu. This is the first night I've been allowed out. I went to a lousy fair—'

'Same here,' I interrupted. 'Still, if you hadn't turned up when you did—'

'You'd have been a goner,' he said cheerfully. 'I'm Colin Butler, by the way.'

'Marcus Howlett, and I can't tell you how pleased I am to meet you.' But my voice still sounded odd and very squeaky. I think it must have been the shock. 'I suppose I ought to stagger home,' I said.

'Do you want me to come with you?' he asked.

'No, but I'd like to chat with you some more tomorrow when I'm feeling more like my old self. So, where do you live?'

'Fourteen, Blake Drive, it's just round—'

'I know it,' I interrupted. 'Well, maybe catch you tomorrow.'

'Sure. Look after yourself, Marcus,' said Colin, and he said this really warmly, as if we were already good mates. Then he added unexpectedly, 'I'd stay in for the next few nights if I were you – I think that bat might come after you again.'

'Sounds like good advice,' I began, but Colin had already darted off home.

I fell inside my house and Mum sent me straight upstairs to get dry. Now she's making me some of her special soup (it has a bit of blood added to it).

Saturday 3 January

10.05 a.m.

I really didn't want to think about all that had gone on last night. I just wanted to go to sleep.

Only the Blood Ghost wouldn't let me.

CHAPTER TWELVE

Saturday 3 January

10.05 a.m.

It kept jumping into my dreams. Or rather its strange twisty hands and rage-filled eyes did. And even when I woke up I couldn't shake it off. The Blood Ghost was still hanging around inside my head. And then I saw a dark shape moving about in my bedroom.

I rubbed my eyes. No, it was still there. But how did it get in? And why did it keep picking on me? This was harassment. I was scared – of course I was. But I was also angry and totally fed up. That's why I tore out of bed and shouted, 'Get out of my bedroom now!'

The dark shape stopped, stood completely

still and turned into my dad saying, 'Hey, Marcus, it's me. Whatever is wrong?'

'You're what's wrong,' I said, 'prowling around my bedroom in the middle of the night. It's like being in the *Big Brother* house living here, except I'm the only contestant. I never get a moment's privacy. You and Mum questioning me about everything.' I hadn't meant to launch into a big rant, but I was so shaken up I didn't quite know what I was saying.

'Now hang on,' said Dad. 'I wasn't prowling about, and it's not the middle of the night either. It's after half past nine in the morning, and you don't normally sleep that long. So I was just looking in on you, that's all.'

'Oh, right. OK, well, that's different then,' I said, feeling more than a bit stupid now.

'But I'll leave you to collect yourself,' he said.

And he did. But he returned a few minutes later with Mum. They both came and sat on the side of my bed. They had their concerned faces on.

'The last day or two,' said Dad, 'we've felt as if you've been somewhere else. Not yourself at all. You're very worried about something, aren't you?'

This was true, but I wasn't at all certain I should admit it.

'We know what it is too,' said Dad.

That gave me a shock, I can tell you.

Dad went on, 'My parents told me about this special power very early on. I tell you, I've never wanted anything so badly. So I was bitterly disappointed when I discovered I didn't have the gift. But you do.'

'And that's wonderful,' cut in Mum.

'Only now you're upset and frustrated it hasn't come through, despite all your hard work, aren't you?' asked Dad.

This was the biggest thing in their life right now, so they just assumed it was the same for me.

'But,' said Dad, 'we don't want you worrying like this. And if for some reason the special power doesn't come through, it's not the end of the world. Well, your mum and I have managed all right.'

'Keep saying the phrases Tara has taught you,' said Mum. 'And keep hoping.'

'But you're not to worry, all right?' said Dad.

'All right,' I agreed.

10.40 a.m.

My parents also told me to stay in bed as long as I liked today – something they'd never normally say. So I put on the radio – and there was the Blood Ghost waiting for me.

Early this morning a guy had gone out for a walk with his dog when the sky seemed to darken and this shadowy figure just tore out of the air at him.

Its hands twisted and turned and the man couldn't stop staring at them, while all the time this big, terrifying shape got nearer. The dog could see it too, growling and snarling at it and then running for its life. While the man fainted (or thought he did).

When he was found he was in a really weak condition. The dreadful shock must have caused that, they were saying on the news. But I knew it was because so much blood had been taken from him.

Now there's a discussion: Is a ghost really haunting us? Or is it just mass hysteria? Two people are having a right old row about it too.

Of course, they're both wrong.

The Blood Ghost is getting busier – and bolder, with another early-morning attack.

Something no vampire would normally attempt.

And this is just the start.

10.55 a.m.

I've sent Cyril a text. Here's what I said:

Hi, Cyril, I got attacked last night about ten
o'clock on the way home from the fair. And
I know for certain the deadly vampire is out
there.

And if I hadn't had help last night from
a boy, also on his way home from the fair, I
wouldn't be able to write this now. In fact,
I'm not even sure I'd be alive.

Glad the fingerprints clinched the
snowman's true identity. Tallulah also thinks
Rathbone the ventriloquist is highly suspicious.
He might be worth checking out. And anyway, it's over to you now, Cyril, as I've got tons
of homework coming up, so I'm resigning
from this case. But let me know when you've
done your stuff.

I really, really wouldn't delay.

Lots of luck,

Marcus

11.10 a.m.

Yeah, I know the homework excuse is pretty lame. But I don't care. I just want him to know I'm out of this now.

11.15 a.m.

Joel's just rung up to ask how I got on with Tallulah. 'It wasn't just that she turned me down, it was that she seemed angry I'd even asked her.'

'Oh, sunshine probably makes her angry,' said Joel. 'And if Tallulah's nice to anyone for more than thirty seconds her head explodes. I'd say you've had a very lucky escape.' Then we went on to talk about something much more important than Tallulah – snow.

Joel's heard that major snowfall is forecast for tomorrow night. Well, it's about time. We didn't get a single flake over Christmas.

11.20 a.m.

Feeling restless.

I just can't settle to anything, so I thought I'd ring Gracie. I can tell her anything.

I even thought I'd tell her about Tallulah.

Get a girl's point of view on it all. But then I stopped and thought, *What am I doing?*

There I was fretting about Tallulah when the perfect girlfriend was here all the time, right in front of my eyes.

Of course. Of course.

Gracie is really pretty, she laughs at my jokes and she likes me. You can sort of tell with most girls, can't you? Plus she's my best friend already. I mean, Joel is too, of course. But I can tell Gracie half-vampire stuff that I can't tell anyone else.

So what more do I want? And why haven't I asked her out before? I'm going to ring her right now.

11.23 a.m.

Would you believe it? Gracie's phone is switched off. She hardly ever does that. And I'm bursting with frustration. I'll definitely try again.

11.45 a.m.

Feeling more restless than ever now. So I've decided to go and see Colin – and thank him properly for what he did last night.

11.55 a.m.

My mum was going to give me the full interrogation about where I was going. But Dad cut in, 'That's all right, Marcus, you go off and enjoy yourself. We're eating about half past one. We know you'll be home by then.'

1.10 p.m.

I found Blake Drive easily. It's one of the roads off what we call the High Street (four shops and a post office). And number 14 was all marked up.

I rang the doorbell and after a while a guy appeared, hair all dishevelled, eyes bleary. He looked a bit too young to be Colin's dad, although I'm hopeless at guessing ages. 'Hi there, is Colin about?' I asked.

The guy squinted at me. 'No one called Colin lives here, mate.'

'Colin Butler,' I repeated.

'You've got the wrong address.'

'This is fourteen Blake Drive?'

Now the guy became a bit curious. 'Someone give you this address then, did they?'

'Yeah, a boy about thirteen.'

'He must have been messing you about, as

no boy lives here. It's just me and my mum. It has been for years.' He gave me a puzzled look and then closed the door.

This didn't make sense. I couldn't have got that address wrong – I'd even put it on my mobile. And Colin wouldn't deliberately give me the wrong address. What would be the point of doing that?

Then the door of number 14 opened again and a woman rushed over to me. 'Excuse me,' she said, 'but I'm Mrs Edwards and I hear you're looking for a boy called Colin.'

'Yeah, that's right. I met him last night – and he helped me. So I wanted to thank him. But I've obviously got the wrong address.'

She was really staring at me now as she announced, 'I've lived here for nine years, but before me there was a family and they had a son called Colin.'

I felt the breath catch in my throat.

'Only he died very suddenly. The poor lad was only thirteen too.'

CHAPTER THIRTEEN

Saturday 3 January

1.15 p.m.

I was so stunned I couldn't reply, while Mrs Edwards went on talking.

'The Butlers moved away shortly after their son died. Well, I suppose there were just too many memories here.'

Her own son was standing close beside her now, eyeballing me very suspiciously. 'So,' he said, 'this Colin died over nine years ago – yet you claim you saw him last night. Now what's that all about?'

The shock had made my mind freeze up. So, gabbling wildly, I said, 'Someone's played a trick on me, that's what it is. Just wait until I get my hands on them, spooking me up like this. Anyway, great to meet you both, let's do this again. Now I know where you live I can pop along. Well, not too soon, don't want to make a nuisance of myself.' I laughed loudly then, but I was the only one.

They were both gaping at me in a distinctly alarmed sort of way now. Still laughing crazily, I darted away. Then I half ran about in a demented sort of way for a few minutes, not knowing what I was doing.

I really hadn't seen that one coming at all.

I just thought Colin was this top new mate, who'd helped me out when I needed it most. Instead . . . well, I suppose he could be a loon who went about pretending to be a boy who died nine years ago.

But then I had a flash of memory from last night. I was soaked through, but the rain hadn't touched Colin.

He wasn't wet at all.

A tiny little detail, totally overshadowed by everything else that had happened – until now.

So yes, Colin probably was a ghost.

Knowing that made me feel shivery and sad and funny. Not funny ha-ha – but funny highly peculiar, as if nothing was solid. Actually, if the pavement had suddenly risen up in the air and thrown me off I wouldn't have been totally surprised. I couldn't trust anything right now.

In the end I plonked myself down on this bench outside the post office. Never in my life sat there before. But I did today – and for so long I was worried birds would start perching on me and building their nests.

Before I got up, and as no one was about, I said softly, 'Colin, it's highly unlikely you can hear this. You've probably floated off to wherever ghosts normally hang out. But I'll never forget how you helped me last night. And I so wish you were alive now.'

Then I got up and went home.

1.23 p.m.

On the way back I rang Gracie again. But her phone was still turned off. Talk about inconsiderate.

3.40 p.m.

Just had a text from Cyril, asking me to call round and see him urgently. He can't have read my text very carefully – especially the bit where I said I'd resigned from this case. And the very last thing I want is to see him again (I don't like him much anyway). And he's got the proof about the snowman. So it's really up to him now. I'm going to totally ignore that text.

5.20 p.m.

A few minutes ago my parents popped over to a neighbour's house. They make a really big deal of being friendly with the neighbours and fitting in. So I crashed out in my room. I felt dead tired, even though I hadn't done much today.

Then I heard something smash against my window. I jumped up – my first (and second) thought was *deadly vampires*. But then I figured even they wouldn't start throwing stones.

But someone was doing just that.

Whack. Another stone hit my window.

I pushed open the window and shouted,

'Look, stop throwing stones at my window, whoever you are. It's not funny – it's just pathetic.'

Someone shouted back, 'Sorry, but I had to get your attention fast – I'm on the run.'

It was Gracie.

CHAPTER FOURTEEN

Saturday 3 January

5.25 p.m.

Gracie was at my front door with a large bag and wearing a huge floppy hat and sunglasses.

I stared at her.

'I wanted to make sure I wasn't noticed,' she explained.

'Oh, yeah – and wearing sunglasses in January is a great way of doing that. So why exactly are you on the run?'

'You don't sound very pleased to see me.'

'Of course I am. It's just – what's going on, Gracie?'

'Your parents are out, aren't they?' said Gracie.

'Yeah, yeah.'

'They must never know I'm here.'

'Even more intriguing. Look, come in.'

'I was wondering when you were going to say that,' said Gracie.

Once inside Gracie handed me two large bars of chocolate. 'Here's my advance thank-you gift. You can never have too much chocolate, can you?'

'You certainly can't. But what are you thanking me for?'

At last she explained. 'On Tuesday, or Wednesday if I'm very lucky, I'll have an attack of what my mum calls "challenging hair". This is one of the extra fun things us girl half-vampires have,' she went on, her voice bubbling with sarcasm. 'This challenging hair will cover my whole body . . .'

'You're going to make the wolf man look clean-shaven.'

'Exactly, and it lasts for two whole weeks.'

'Hey, that's awful.'

'I know, and anyway, my mum thinks I should spend these last few precious hours of freedom preparing myself – which means listening to her telling me over and over how she got through her challenging hair phase. And I can't stand that. I have to do something. Anything. And then I read about the Winter Fair here.'

'Oh, yeah?' I muttered unenthusiastically.

'And I thought, *I'll catch a train here and run away so I can go to the fair – which isn't very far from my good mate Marcus*. I can hide away in your shed.'

'Have you seen the size of our shed? Even the spiders complain about over-crowding. No, you can live in the wardrobe in my bedroom. You can sleep standing up and breathe very quietly, can't you?'

'Of course, can't everyone?'

I grinned at her. 'And how long are you planning on residing in my wardrobe?'

'Well, I thought until Tuesday – I suppose you are back at school on Monday . . . ?'

'Yeah, unfortunately, but I can skive off with pleasure.'

'No, don't do that. I'll go round the shops or to the cinema or something. Then on Monday night we could sneak off somewhere else. You can choose, this time. And after that I suppose I'll have to give myself up, as the attack of challenging hair will strike. But not until then. So it's vital my mum doesn't know I'm here – though later I will send her a text saying I'm safe, so she doesn't worry too much. I know I should have warned you I was coming. But I thought you might try and talk me out of it. You will help me, won't you? And go to the fair with me tonight?'

I looked at Gracie, still in her sunglasses and absurd hat. 'This is the maddest, craziest scheme I've ever heard . . . so, of course I will.'

6.15 p.m.

Gracie's had a shower and unpacked all her stuff into the bottom drawer of my wardrobe. 'I feel as if I'm here on my holidays,' she giggled.

Then my parents came back. 'I'll go down and entertain them,' I said. 'You just chill out here.' I switched my music up loud before I left and closed the door tightly.

Downstairs Dad peered at me. 'You seem more your old self.'

'Yeah, I am. By the way, I'm starving.'

I cunningly stuffed some sandwiches into my pocket and delivered them to Gracie. The sandwiches were generously decorated with all the bits of stuff that live in my pockets. But she said they were delicious anyway, as they tasted of freedom.

6.25 p.m.

Dad's sloshing about in the shower now, totally unaware that Gracie is next door to him. When he started singing, this massive laugh just exploded out of Gracie.

Dad called out, 'You all right, Marcus?'

'Yeah, Dad,' I replied. 'I just sneezed, that's all.'

6.28 p.m.

I tell you, having someone staying illegally in your house makes you forget all your worries. I'd highly recommend it.

6.55 p.m.

I told my parents I was popping out for a bit. Dad's still trying hard to be laid back, so he just said, 'Good to see you looking more cheerful. We know you'll come back at a reasonable hour.'

As I was leaving I heard the phone ring. It was Gracie's mum, no doubt reporting Gracie's disappearance. I slipped away before my parents could start questioning me. I switched my mobile off too.

And while I'd been chatting to my parents I'd left the front door open. So Gracie was already some way ahead of me. We were very careful not to meet up until we were right away from my house.

CHAPTER FIFTEEN

Saturday 3 January

7.50 p.m.

I strolled off to the fair with Gracie feeling positively carefree. Yeah, I was returning to the Winter Fair, but the snowman wouldn't be there as Cyril had the proof he needed and would certainly have challenged him by now. After which the snowman would have shrivelled away with shame.

I was just here tonight to have some fun with my new girlfriend. I hadn't actually asked Gracie out yet. But I would very soon – only not on the ghost train. In fact, that's one place I wouldn't go near.

Then, as the fair loomed, I saw a familiar

figure capering about and laughing even more loudly at his own jokes. Red-hot shock rushed through me.

I was boiling with anger too. That snowman was extremely dangerous. Cyril had told us that – so why hadn't he done anything? Did it have anything to do with that text he'd sent me earlier? It must have – but what? I sort of wished I'd seen Cyril now.

And then the person who last night had tried to drain me of every drop of blood I possessed thumped over to us. His eyes were as cold and dead as before.

'Can't keep away from us, can you?' he shouted.

I just wanted to explode with frustration that he was still on the loose. But instead I snapped, 'Well, it was a choice between watching paint dry or coming here. You very narrowly won.' Then, seeing Gracie watching all this, I murmured, 'I'm just here for a quiet night.'

'Oh, you won't get any peace here,' said the snowman firmly. 'None at all.' He rolled nearer to me and I got a whiff of his pongy aftershave. I'd smelled it before, of course – off Mr Rathbone. Was it just a coincidence they both had the same hideous taste?

But then I remembered something else. That horrible screeching noise I'd heard last night, just before the Blood Ghost appeared. It had reminded me of someone. Now I think I knew whose voice it was – Mr Rathbone's, when he was pretending to be Hugo.

I'd probably need to hear Rathbone's voice again to be absolutely certain. But if I were certain – did that mean there were two deadly vampires here already?

My skin prickled. For these deadly vampires to vanish we'd need to expose both of them.

But I still couldn't believe it. Two of them already.

Then I noticed Gracie staring at me.

'What!' I grinned, desperately trying to recapture the carefree mood of before.

'You looked at that snowman as if you totally hated him.'

'Yeah, well, I was frightened by a snowman when I was a baby. Never liked them since.'

Then it was our turn to pay up and get our hands stamped. But Gracie walked into the fair looking surprisingly glum.

'Hey, what's up?' I asked.

'I just really hate it when people lie to me, especially someone I thought was a good friend.'

'You don't mean me.'

'Tell me the real reason why you and the snowman were exchanging evil glances. Or don't bother speaking.'

'You really want to know?'

'Yes, I really do.'

'I know something about him.'

'What?'

'Not here.' I pointed. 'We can talk up there.'

A couple of minutes later Gracie and I were strapped into the big wheel. Then as it groaned into the air, leaving the fair noises behind, I started telling her about yesterday, the vampire attacks, and being rescued by Colin. I'd planned to miss out the bit about asking Tallulah out. Well, it wasn't very important and later when I got round to asking Gracie out, she might think I was doing it on the rebound.

But in the end I even filled her in on that. It took a while, though – four journeys on the big wheel, in fact.

Finally we staggered away.

And Gracie said, 'I'm frightened for you . . . What if that boy ghost hadn't turned up last night . . . ?' She didn't finish that sentence and just stopped walking, while crowds jostled round us. Then, looking right at me, she asked, 'What do you want to happen now, Marcus?'

For once I didn't make a silly comment or joke. I said, 'More than anything else I just want to get out of this. But instead . . . well, I really thought the snowman would be gone by now. Why's he still here, Gracie?'

'Because he's in this with Rathbone? And they'll only disappear when Cyril rounds them both up.'

'That's possible, I suppose.'

'So we need' – she lowered her voice to a whisper – 'to find the other deadly vampire, and you practically have. I think we should go back to that phoney fortune-teller.'

'No way,' I began.

'Hear me out. I'll go along and have my fortune told. You just listen to the ventriloquist's voice once more. And if it is the same voice you heard last night then you've definitely got him. You can text Cyril that there are two DVs, not one as he thought, and he must confront them both. And if he does that they could be gone by – well, later on tonight. Wouldn't that be fantastic?'

'Fantastic is a total understatement. But I don't want to involve you in all this.'

'Don't be silly. All I'll do is ask him to tell my fortune. My part's easy and completely safe.'

Then Gracie said, 'Look, there's Tallulah.'

I glanced over for a second. Yeah, there she was, lurking about more than a bit obviously. I didn't know what she was up to – and didn't care. So I quickly turned away.

'Tallulah? Never heard of her.' And actually, only a very small stabbing pain ran through my heart. So I was getting over her – and last night's total humiliation – with great speed really.

Gracie linked our arms and said, 'By the way, I think she was mad turning you down.'

'Do you?' So here was my chance to ask her out. The words were on the tip of my tongue when I saw it – the beginnings of a moustache around the right side of Gracie's mouth.

But it couldn't be. Not yet. Gracie had two more days at least before this happened. Maybe the scrap of a moustache was just a preview of coming attractions. A kind of trailer. It didn't mean any more would be sprouting up anytime soon, did it?

So I quickly decided it didn't, and I wouldn't tell Gracie as that would absolutely kill her big night of freedom. And what did a little facial hair matter anyway – it was kind of cute, really. So instead, still arm in arm (and I so hoped Tallulah was watching us) we wandered to the ventriloquist's tent.

Gracie peered at the picture outside. 'I'd say that is the most sinister-looking ventriloquist's dummy I've ever seen.'

But I wasn't really looking at the picture, I was studying Gracie. Was that moustache growing a bit thicker? I wasn't completely sure at first. Then I decided it definitely wasn't.

'Ready, then?' said Gracie.

'If you're sure . . . ?' I asked.

'I'm positive.'

There was a different boy outside. I paid three pounds for Gracie to have her hand read and then we stepped inside.

'It's very dark in here,' whispered Gracie.

'That's so you can't see what a lousy ventriloquist Mr Rathbone is,' I said.

As before it was the dummy who greeted us, calling out, 'It's that boy again, the one who came to see us last night. Only he's with a completely different girl today. Should I say anything?'

I suppose that might have been amusing, but actually it just sounded rude and nasty. That's the thing about deadly vampires – the snowman is another example – however hard they try and be funny they just never are. So there's another way you can spot a vampire, I suppose. Not only no heart but no real sense of humour, either.

Then the ventriloquist spoke. 'Hugo, you must be quiet. We're delighted to welcome visitors for a second time – and whoever they choose to bring with them.'

'Crawler! Crawler!' yelled Hugo.

And it was then something snapped in my head. That ventriloquist was very skilled at altering his voice. Well, I suppose that was his job. But I heard it then all right. A distinct echo of the Blood Ghost's call last night.

Mr Rathbone was, without doubt, a deadly vampire too.

CHAPTER SIXTEEN

Saturday 3 January

8.30 p.m.

I sat so still my feet might have been stuck to the floor. I shouldn't really have been shocked. I'd been practically certain Rathbone was the other deadly vampire before. But having to sit facing him and his bleakly unfunny dummy made it all seem terrifyingly real.

And again I wondered how I was ever going to get out of all this. It was like those films where people are caught in quicksand and the more they struggle, the worse it gets. Well, as soon as we were out of there I'd text Cyril what I knew. He got me into all this danger. So it was up to him to get me out – and fast.

But I was determined Gracie wouldn't be dragged into this any further. Let Rathbone think she was just a casual friend. I didn't want him knowing anything else about her.

And then another thought struck me. Vampires can quickly suss out who's a half-vampire, can't they? And they love exposing us. So had Rathbone already worked out Gracie's secret identity? No, not in here. He could hardly even see her. But I was still worried. And I so wished I'd never brought Gracie here and that the whole fortune-telling was over.

And then it was, before it had even really started. Gracie sprang up and said in such an odd voice, 'I'm sorry, but I feel very faint. Got to go.'

I jumped up after her.

'Not again. What happens to you and your girlfriends?' yelled Hugo, as unfunny as ever.

'*You* happen,' I said. 'And you're just the worst thing imaginable.'

I absolutely shouldn't have said that. I was giving away all my suspicions of him, although Hugo just laughed as if I'd made a joke. That was the last sound I heard in that tent – Hugo's mocking laugh.

Outside Gracie was standing with her hand half covering her face. 'I'm sorry,' she said. 'Have I messed everything up?'

'No, not at all.'

'Did you recognize his voice?'

'Yeah, I did,' I said softly.

'Oh, good – so you can tell Cyril?'

'Yeah.'

Then she said, 'It's started . . . did you know?'

'That you've got a very slight case of facial hairiness? Yeah, I did, but I hoped it was the slow-growing kind.'

'No, once it starts . . . I just suddenly felt this itchiness on my face and reached up. I've got a moustache sprouting up on the right side of my face, haven't I?'

I quickly checked.

'Yes, that is true. But there is some good news too, and here it is: the left side of your face is smooth and attractive. In fact, it's probably the smoothest, most attractive left side of a face I've ever seen.'

'That could change any second, though. Marcus, don't let anyone see me.'

'No, because if they do they'll all be madly jealous. In fact, you'll probably start a trend. Girls all over the country will be going to parties with half a moustache plastered on. They'll even call it "doing a Gracie".' I was babbling all this while putting an arm round Gracie and clasping her very tightly. I could feel her shaking and thought at first she was laughing. But then I realized she was crying, but very silently.

She whispered softly, 'This isn't who I want to be.'

I could feel all her sadness and frustration and totally understood it. I held her even more tightly and whispered, 'I know, but this is the very worst bit. If you can get through this – and you definitely will – well, then . . . how would you like to be my girlfriend?'

'You pick the oddest moments to ask girls to go out with you.'

'I'd even say I have a talent for it. But I've been meaning to ask you out . . .'

'Ever since Tallulah turned you down,' said Gracie with a teasing smile.

'No, it's always been you, really. It's just I only realized it today because I'm a total idiot. So what do you say – yes, or yes?'

'I say, ask me again when I'm not turning into Wolf Girl. Do you promise you will? Say it now.'

'I promise I will ask you again.'

'Thanks – no one's looking at me, are they?'

'I've totally camouflaged you and it's an exceptionally dark night.' And it was. A black sky hung over us and it was starting to rain again now.

'But soon they'll see me all right, no matter how dark it gets. I'll have to ring my mum. Get ready for an almighty ear-bashing.'

After she'd called her mum, Gracie made me text Cyril that I'd definitely located the other deadly vampire. Then we waited outside the fair for Gracie's mum in the deepest shadows as the hair was starting to sprout on the left side of Gracie's face as well now.

'Promise that when you think of me,' said Gracie, 'it won't be like this.'

'Who says I'm going to be thinking of you at all?' I grinned.

And then Gracie's mum tore towards us as if she were auditioning to be a stunt driver. For a mad moment I thought she might even run us both over.

Gracie didn't rush into her mum's car as I'd expected. And her mum didn't get out either. Instead, she bellowed through the window, 'You stupid, stupid girl! I said it could begin early.'

'Shout a bit louder, Mum,' cried Gracie. 'I'm sure there are a couple of people at the fair who haven't heard you yet.'

'You left without a word and I've been worrying myself to death. And you,' she went on, suddenly pulling me into the conversation, 'shouldn't have encouraged her.'

'He didn't,' snapped Gracie. 'I just turned up at his house. Anything to get away from you.'

This certainly wasn't the most tender reunion I'd ever seen. And things didn't improve when Gracie's mum just erupted out of the car and came storming over to us, while yelling at me, 'Well, help me get her into the car. You may as well do something useful.'

'Yeah, sure,' I said.

'Oh, just throw a paper bag over my head, I'll be fine,' said Gracie. But her mum and I ignored this. No one was actually watching us, but we both blocked out even the tiniest glimpse of her face. And we guided Gracie towards the car as if we'd just blindfolded her.

As Gracie sat in the back seat, I grabbed hold of her hand. She squeezed it back. 'See you soon,' she whispered.

'You can count on that.'

'I also have a message for you from your parents,' snapped Gracie's mum. 'They said you've to go home right away as they have much to say to you.'

'I can't wait,' I muttered.

'Do you want a lift?' asked Gracie. 'We'll have to go back to your house to get my stuff.'

'There's no time for that now,' said Gracie's mum. 'I'll have to pick it up tomorrow.'

'That's fine, you two get off,' I said.

'Yes, I rather think we'd better,' said Gracie's mum, driving away as wildly as she'd arrived, with Gracie crouched down and hidden away from everyone.

9.20 p.m.

I didn't want to go home, yet I couldn't hang around at the fair any more either. It was unnerving me too much. Especially as more than once I had the feeling I was being trailed.

I didn't actually see anyone, but you know how you can sense when someone is watching you. Was the snowman secretly observing me? I hadn't seen him lumbering about recently.

Or maybe he'd gone at last. My hopes rose until I heard him laughing so loudly it was like a mini-volcano. I figured I'd rather get an ear-bashing from my parents than have to listen to that sound again. So I fled.

9.25 p.m.

I was too unnerved to take the short cut through Brent Woods. So I went home the long way, walking along this narrow pathway by the main road. It was even darker now, with only the lights from the cars whizzing past. They roared past me and then one crazy driver went so fast he actually skidded against the narrow pavement. But he quickly recovered and tore off even faster.

What a mad driver, I thought. Then I forgot all about it until I saw something moving slowly along the side of the pavement. At first, I thought it was a deer which had been hit by that crazy driver.

But as I got closer I saw it was a man in a suit, dragging himself along the ground with his hands. He was choking and coughing too. I sped forward to help him.

But then I wondered if it was a trap. Was that odd crawling figure merely a disguise for the deadly vampire? And when I knelt down would it suddenly transform into a bat?

I really didn't know – though I knew I couldn't just leave him. I had to find out. So I kept on running, but then the figure must have seen me as he stopped moving – and croaked out my name.

And then I could see who it was – Cyril.

CHAPTER SEVENTEEN

Saturday 3 January

9.25 p.m. (cont'd)

'Hey, this is terrible,' I gabbled. 'That car hit you, didn't it? Look, I'll pull you up.'

'I'd much rather you didn't pull at me,' said Cyril, snotty as ever, even in a situation like this. 'I suffer from severe back problems as it is.' So instead I slowly dragged him to his feet. It took ages. After which he took a few steps back and I was afraid he was going to fall down again. He looked remarkably unsteady.

I grabbed hold of his arm and asked, 'That car went zigzagging onto the pavement deliberately, didn't it?'

'Of course it did,' said Cyril. 'That's obvious to anyone. In some ways these vampires are like medieval gangsters.'

'So it was a deadly vampire driving that car?'

'Well, he didn't have a flashing sign attached to his head saying "I'm a deadly vampire", but I'm pretty certain he was one.'

Somehow Cyril always made me feel stupid – even when I'd just rescued him. 'And where have you been?' I asked.

Cyril looked surprised by the question. 'To the fair, of course.' Only Cyril could go to the fair in a suit. He'd probably strut about the beach in one too. 'As you declined to contact me I came to see if I could find you at the fair. I was, of course, unsuccessful. But I did visit the ventriloquist Tallulah was so suspicious of.' He paused. 'Like my uncle, I have a nose for vampires and I suspected him right away. Unfortunately, I think he also suspected me. I told you how my uncle and his investigations are well known to vampires. You might even call us very reluctant celebrities.' Cyril started brushing himself down. 'Of course, I had no clinching proof of the ventriloquist's identity until this shabby attack on me.'

'Here's a bit more proof for you,' I said. 'I recognized Rathbone's voice just before the attack last night. He was there too. I'm certain of it. I sent you a text . . .'

Cyril squinted at me. 'You've had quite a time.'

'Yeah, I've made loads of new enemies.'

'And the idea of two deadly vampires working together . . .' He paused.

'That's not good,' I said.

'It's unusual – and very serious,' he sighed. 'And I'm so exhausted already.'

I didn't see why. It wasn't as if he'd done much.

He rang for a taxi and then said he wanted to know everything that had happened to me last night.

Cyril didn't interrupt once until I mentioned the boy who'd come to my rescue. It was when I said his name – Colin Butler – that he had a kind of convulsion. 'What did you say?' he asked in a strange, choked voice.

'Colin Butler, and the thing was—'

'He was a ghost,' he interrupted.

'How on earth do you know that?' I demanded.

'You remember I mentioned someone was killed nine years ago by the deadly vampires, the first time they tried draining humans of blood? Well, it was a thirteen-year-old boy called . . . Colin Butler.'

Cold with shock, I could only stare at him.

'Very few humans knew that, of course,' said Cyril. 'Only us experts. But Uncle Giles is convinced that's what happened. He also believes it was a huge mistake. They'd meant to target Colin Butler's best friend.'

'But surely it wouldn't have mattered whose blood they took.'

'Not normally, but it would have done in this case,' said Cyril, 'because Colin Butler wasn't a human at all. He was a half-vampire.'

CHAPTER EIGHTEEN

Saturday 3 January

9.25 p.m. (cont'd)

That was another massive shock. But somehow I recovered quickly and asked, 'A half-vampire – whatever is that?'

'Haven't you ever heard of them?' asked Cyril.

'Never,' I said firmly.

'You surprise me,' said Cyril. 'I even wondered if you had a distant relation who was one.'

A million alarm bells went off in my head at once. Reluctant half-vampire that I was, I knew how vital it was to keep my identity top secret at all times. Nothing was more important than that. And yet here was Cyril – well, he was just fishing right now. But this was serious. I couldn't let any human break my cover.

Cyril moved closer to me. 'I just wondered if Colin Butler, whom Uncle Giles is certain was a half-vampire, was helping someone else with – shall we say – half-vampire connections.'

'What total rubbish,' I cried loudly.

Cyril said in a low voice, 'It's always been one of my ambitions to meet someone who can tell me about half-vampires.'

'Well, I can't, as I've never heard of them,' I said.

'Are you sure?'

'Of course I am, and if you don't stop spouting all this rubbish I'm just going to walk off.'

That silenced Cyril – temporarily – so then I rushed on, 'And anyway, I've got some questions for you now. I've brought you definite proof that there's not one but two deadly vampires here. You say it is unusual for vampires to act together.'

'Highly unusual,' said Cyril.

'So when are you going to do something about it, then?'

'Soon.'

'Why not tonight?'

'When I can hardly stand up?'

'Take your walking stick. You could save people – yeah, including me – a whole load of misery if you make that deadly duo go tonight.'

'The thing is,' said Cyril, 'I need back-up.'

'Why?' I demanded.

'I think it would be better.'

'Ring up your Uncle Giles then.'

'He's still not at all well.'

'Well, you'll have to go alone then. It should only take you a few seconds to expose and shame him.'

Cyril still hesitated.

'Or are you afraid?'

'Oh yes, I'm afraid,' said Cyril. 'Any sane person would be afraid of these deadly vampires. These Blood Ghost experiments are proving highly successful. Soon they'll be able to attack humans at any time of the day or night. And like I said, I believe more deadly vampires will be arriving here very,

very soon. And they're planning something really big here in Great Walden.'

'Well, do something then,' I practically shouted. 'And—' I stopped. 'Did you just hear something?' I asked.

'No, I didn't,' he said firmly.

But I did. And once again I had the strongest feeling that I was being followed. I actually peered all around.

'I'm not surprised you feel jumpy,' said Cyril. 'I would be too in your position.' I didn't quite know what he meant by that. But before I could reply he said, 'And now I do hear something – my taxi. Where can I drop you?'

I was about to give him my address when panic set in again. Cyril had tried to guess my most important secret. Of course, he had no real proof. He was just playing with the idea really. But did I really want him knowing where I lived as well? He probably knew anyway (Giles did, for certain). But I didn't want to make it ultra-easy for him by taking him right to my door now.

And if he turned up there to have a chat

with my mum and dad about vampires and half-vampires, well, the shame of that would be more than I could bear.

So I said, 'No, you're all right.'

Cyril looked both angry and worried. 'But you can't go roaming about at night.' Then, as if reading my mind, 'You can trust me, you know. I will never tell anyone my vague suspicions – and that's all they are—'

'I don't know what you're talking about,' I interrupted. 'Just send me a text when you've seen off the deadly vampires – and do it very soon.'

11.45 p.m.

Back home – and to my amazement I didn't get an ear-bashing from my parents. They were amused – and even a bit pleased – that I'd helped Gracie. In fact, they were laughing as they helped me pack away her things for her mum to pick up tomorrow.

'And Gracie is absolutely fine now?' said Mum.

'If you can call having your whole body covered in hair for two weeks absolutely fine,' I said.

'Not easy,' said Mum. 'I still remember it all too clearly.'

'Now do tell me,' said Dad, still in a light-hearted mood, 'if you'd brought Gracie back, where would she have slept tonight?'

'Oh, I'd have let her have my bed,' I said, 'and I'd have slept on the floor.'

'Hmm,' said Mum. 'And tomorrow when you went back to school, what would you have done – packed her away in your school bag?'

'What a great idea,' I said. 'Why ever didn't we think of that?'

Mum and Dad looked at each other and then laughed again.

They were being so reasonable and good-humoured about everything that I told them something else. 'By the way,' I said to them, 'I've asked Gracie if she'd like to be my girl-friend.'

'And what did she say?' asked Mum at once.

'She said yes. Well, sort of. I'm to ask her again when she's less hairy. But how can she say no?'

'And she's such a nice girl,' said Mum.

'Now don't go putting me off,' I said. But

my parents looked as if they were about to explode with joy.

'She's right for you,' said Mum.

'Because she's a half-vampire,' I said.

'No, no, not at all . . . but, well, you have got a unique insight into each other's special challenges.'

Then Dad said, 'We've asked Tara, your tutor at—'

'I remember who she is,' I interrupted.

'Good, well, we've asked if she'll come round here on Tuesday evening and give you an extra lesson. But if you'd rather not see her then we'll cancel.'

'Give it some thought first, though,' said Mum, 'because time is—' She stopped.

'Time is what?' I asked.

But Dad's eyes went uneasy and Mum immediately backed off.

But I know exactly how that sentence would have finished: 'Time is running out.'

Actually, I'm certain it's run out for my special power already. So why can't my parents accept that?

I have.

Sunday 4 January

12.15 a.m.

I've just received two texts:

Thanks for everything. Mum has calmed down at last. I'll ring you tomorrow.
   Take great care.
   Love from Wolf Girl
P.S. Did I tell you to take great care?

Just remember, they will definitely try and strike again. You are in very great danger.
   Regards,
   Cyril

CHAPTER NINETEEN

Monday 5 January

12.15 p.m.

Back at school. And what's the first thing I see scribbled on the whiteboard? BEWARE OF THE BLOOD GHOST. Wherever I go I crash into it.

Then at break time a Year Seven boy told us breathlessly how he'd seen the Blood Ghost while he was doing his paper round that morning. 'It started waving its fingers which were dripping with blood. And if I hadn't flung my papers down and run for my life I'd be another of its victims now.'

It sounded more than a bit unlikely to me. But the Year Seven boy had a large crowd listening to his story. Among them was Tallulah. And I hate not talking to people. In fact, I think it's totally pathetic. So I said 'Hi' to her and she said 'Hi' back. She looked as if she wanted to say something else. But I thought it would probably be about the Blood Ghost so I didn't hang about.

4.30 p.m.

I've just rung Gracie. She told me her mum has bought her a new laptop.

'Hey, I'm not feeling sorry for you any more.' I laughed.

'Mum has also taken every mirror down in the whole house.'

'Thoughtful,' I muttered.

Then she said, 'You aren't going back to that fair tonight, are you?'

'No, I'm staying in. My mate Joel's dropping by later, and we might even get some of that snow they've been promising us.'

6.05 p.m.

Another text from Cyril, urging me to be very careful but also saying he'll be away for most of today consulting experts. But

I think he's just putting off the moment when he has to confront those two deadly vampires.

Really, he's scared out of his wits.

6.10 p.m.

I checked with my parents that it was OK if Joel popped round tonight. They said my friends are welcome anytime.

They're being so nice they're starting to freak me out.

8.05 p.m.

The doorbell rang just before eight. I called out to my parents, 'That'll be Joel, I'll get it.'

And it was Joel. Only there was someone standing on the step beside him.

'Yeah, yeah, it's me,' said Tallulah.

My stomach gave a thump, just as if someone had whacked me on the back.

'She's not with me,' cut in Joel. 'I just saw her hanging about here.'

'What do you want?' I asked her.

'It's just a social call really. See, I'll try anything once,' said Tallulah. 'So, aren't you going to invite us in?'

'Yeah, I guess . . .' I said weakly. It was only when Tallulah was inside that I started imagining my parents' reaction. I was banned from even hanging around with Tallulah, let alone having her drop by. So they'd go ballistic. Luckily they were in the sitting room, totally unaware of my unexpected visitor – for now.

But for how long? Again I had this terrible sinking feeling in my stomach. And yet I was also buzzing with curiosity and – yeah, all right – excitement.

What was Tallulah really doing here?

More soon.

8.55 p.m.

So there we were in my bedroom – Tallulah, Joel and me. But Tallulah hovered by the door, as if she was just here to deliver a message.

Then she said quickly, 'I just wanted to say, Marcus, how sorry—'

'Do you want me to leave?' interrupted Joel.

'No,' I said.

'Great,' said Joel, jumping onto my bed, 'because I can't wait to hear this – and don't let me put you off apologizing, Tallulah.'

'Yeah, apologize away, I deserve it,' I said. 'Joel knows how you reacted when I asked you out, by the way.'

'So over to you,' said Joel, 'and speak up, will you? I'm having a little bit of trouble hearing you.'

'Try speaking from your stomach,' I said.

Joel and I were being so snotty, I fully expected Tallulah to exit fast. Part of me wanted that, and for Tallulah to feel just a bit of the humiliation and pain that was still lurking inside me.

But she wasn't put off. In fact, she moved further into my room. She had guts, I'll give her that.

'Are we allowing Tallulah to sit down in your presence?' asked Joel.

'Yes, I think she may – but only for a minute,' I said.

'I'm totally fine standing,' said Tallulah with a flash of her old defiance. She went on, 'That night on the ghost train I acted so stupidly. You didn't deserve that. But you took me completely by surprise. Boys don't normally ask me out.'

'That's true,' said Joel.

'But you weren't so much surprised as . . . steaming with anger when I asked you out.'

'No, I wasn't angry at all,' said Tallulah.

'Believe me, you were,' I said.

'Excuse me,' interrupted Joel, 'but I think Tallulah's face just naturally looks as if she's chewing a wasp.'

'What I'm really saying,' said Tallulah, looking right at me now and ignoring Joel, 'is I would like to go out with you, if the offer is still on.'

'What a touching scene,' said Joel. 'I may cry, or be sick on the carpet.'

Tallulah coming round like this should have meant the world to me. But something didn't feel quite right here. Why the sudden change of heart? Was there more to this than she was saying? There was also the small detail that I'd asked Gracie out now.

Tallulah – and Joel – were looking expectantly at me now.

'Thanks for coming round, Tallulah,' I said slowly, flatly.

'And your comments have been noted,' added Joel.

Then Mum opened the door. 'Good evening, Joel,' she began, but her gracious hostess smile just dived off her face when she saw who else was here. 'Oh, hello, Tallulah,' she said. 'Could I just see you for a moment outside, Marcus?'

'Certainly, Mother,' I said.

Outside, Mum glared furiously at me. 'What's she doing here? And after we expressly told you . . .'

'She arrived with Joel,' I said.

'And what's he doing with her? Does he like her?'

'Yeah, I think he does.'

'But he's already got a girlfriend.'

'He does know that.'

Mum sucked air through her teeth. 'Is this part of that "personal problem" you told us about? Well, all I can say is that he's a very confused young man.'

He wasn't the only one. 'Look, Mum, I had to let her in but she's not staying long.'

'She'd better not be,' said Mum. 'I shall be up again in five minutes.'

Back in my bedroom Joel was standing up and saying, 'Well, I can see you two little rascals have a lot to talk over, so I'm going to push off now. See you, Tallulah.'

I followed Joel outside. He was laughing so

hard he nearly fell over. 'Can you believe her tonight? She's totally bonkers, of course.'

'No, I wouldn't say that,' I said.

Joel's laughter quickly faded away. He slapped me on the back and said, 'Well, if she's the one you want, mate – it looks like you're in luck.'

Tallulah was standing up again when I returned to my bedroom. 'So you want to go out with me now,' I said. 'Bit of a sudden change.'

'Not really – like I said, you took me by surprise before. But I went to the fair last night because I thought you might be there. You must have noticed me hanging about.'

'Yeah, I did.'

'You were with Gracie, weren't you?'

'That's right. Great girl,' I couldn't resist adding. Then I said slowly, 'So you went to the fair last night just to apologize to me?'

'I really did. I was practically stalking you, actually.'

That's why I'd sensed someone was trailing me last night. Someone *had* been – Tallulah. The thought of her making all that effort made me swell with pride and – OK, I'll admit it – happiness.

And she was smiling at me now as she said, 'You're not like anyone else at our school.'

Tallulah was paying me her highest compliment now. It should have been a great moment and it was – until I had a sudden jarring thought. *'You're not like anyone else at our school.'* Was there a particular reason for her saying that?

Like something she'd overheard last night?

'Tallulah, after I left the fair, did you go on following me?' Something in my tone gave her a jolt, and she actually hesitated. 'You did go on following me, didn't you?' I persisted.

'Yes.' She said the word so fast it sounded more like a tiny sneeze.

'And you saw me talking to Cyril, didn't you?'

She was peering intently at the carpet now. 'I think I did, yeah.'

'And did you overhear what we were talking about?'

'Just bits of conversation. Not all of it.'

'Come on, no more games, Tallulah. What exactly did you hear?'

CHAPTER TWENTY

Monday 5 January

8.55 p.m.

Tallulah spoke very slowly now, like someone just awakening from a dream.

'I heard him say you'd been attacked by a vampire,' she paused. 'By the way, why didn't you tell me that?'

'Because I didn't want you to worry about me,' I said, with more than a trace of sarcasm in my voice. 'What else?'

'A boy helped you. Only he was a ghost.'

'You heard a lot. Go on.'

'Cyril reckoned the boy was a half-vampire.'

'And . . . ?' I prompted, my heart thumping furiously now.

Then the words burst out of her in a rush. 'Cyril thinks you might have relatives who've been half-vampires too, which is just about the most exciting thing I've ever heard. Like I said, I always sensed you were different to everyone else, but still, this news is brilliant.'

She was looking at me now as if I were someone really exciting – the way I'd always dreamed of her looking at me. But a girl who likes me just because she suspects I might have connections to half-vampires is not the one for me.

I said wearily, 'Sorry to disillusion you, but Cyril was talking complete and total rubbish. Something he's very skilled at. Actually, I've never even heard of half-vampires.' I paused for a second. 'Now, do you still want to go out with me?'

Before Tallulah could reply, Mum stomped into my bedroom without even pretending to knock, as she normally does. 'You really have a great deal of homework to do, Marcus.'

That was total rubbish. I'd only been back one day and hadn't got any homework yet (and anyway, I never go to bed before 3 a.m. so I had hours and hours yet). But I knew

Mum was hinting – and not at all subtly – that Tallulah must leave now.

'And they're forecasting heavy snow tonight,' she said to Tallulah. The atmosphere was arctic enough for snow in here too. 'It's already started snowing,' she added, before sweeping out. But she didn't go downstairs. Instead, I could hear her bustling about on the landing. Then she switched on a radio. It was so loud the newsreader's voice boomed right into my bedroom.

'Is anything up with your mum?' began Tallulah, but then she stopped talking. We both did. It was the news. And there'd been another attack by the Blood Ghost. That wasn't how they announced it, of course. They said an elderly lady claimed to have seen the Blood Ghost. Only this time she'd been so shocked she had collapsed and was now in a serious but stable condition in hospital.

'That's terrible,' I said.

'And where's Cyril?' asked Tallulah. 'I know he says he's consulting experts. But sometimes I wonder if he's just run away.'

'So do I,' I said.

'And someone's going to be killed soon. I know they are.'

'Tell Cyril.'

'And they're going to try and attack you again.'

'And you'd just hate for anything to happen to me!'

'Of course I would.'

'Oh, you would now, after some mad imaginings from Cyril, the cowardly vampire fighter.'

'That's not fair,' said Tallulah. 'I was already looking for you before, at the fair.'

'In a very half-hearted sort of way.'

'Not at all.'

'Look, the reason you're round here, practically on your knees, is nothing to do with me. It's because of some wild theory of Cyril's you think you overheard. You and he really do belong together, you know. In fact, why don't you pop round to his house now? He might even be back. You'll probably find him cowering under his bed.'

Tallulah shook her head. 'I'm going back to the fair right now. I'll do what Cyril's too afraid to do.'

A chill ran through me. 'No,' I began.

'Yes,' she said, 'because it's not so hard to

get a deadly vampire to leave. We know that. You just tell him, "The game's up," and you taunt him by saying you know who he really is. Then he's so overcome with shame he just shrivels away. Like that other deadly vampire did when you confronted her. Remember?'

'Of course I do. Only Cyril reckons he needs back-up this time.'

'No, Cyril's bottled out,' said Tallulah. 'So I'm doing it instead.' Then she asked, 'Will you come with me?'

'No way,' I said.

'Go on.'

'Look, wait until tomorrow and see if Cyril—'

'No, I can't wait another day.' She said this so firmly I looked at her.

'What are you talking about now?' I asked.

'Next week,' she said, 'I've got to go away to some stupid sanatorium.'

My heart jumped into my mouth. 'So your illness . . . ?'

'Yeah, it's still hanging around. And they are having great difficulty in diagnosing the cause of it. So some other doctors have got to see me to do still more tests and try to isolate the bug or something like that. And I'm supposed to be getting ready for it – by lying in bed resting. Have you ever heard anything more stupid?' She moved closer to me. 'Marcus, I've seen my future and it's so boring it's yawning at me. But if I send those deadly vampires packing tonight, well, I honestly don't care what happens to me after that – only, please come with me.'

Everything went still for a moment then, just as it had when I'd asked Tallulah out two nights ago. Only now it was me saying no. I had no choice, did I? I couldn't get pulled into this any more.

Tallulah, looking more than a bit deflated, turned to leave.

'You mustn't go there either. It's a crazy idea,' I called after her.

She turned round. 'But crazy ideas are the only ones I like,' she added. 'Just checking – but are we are going out together now?'

'No. You see, I asked another girl out last night.'

'Was it Gracie?'

'Yeah – it's Gracie.' There was an awkward silence for a moment, then, 'You've met her, haven't you?' I asked.

'Oh yeah, she seems all right,' mumbled Tallulah. 'Bye, then.'

The second Tallulah had left, Mum confronted me in my bedroom. 'Joel hasn't taken up with that girl, has he?'

'Maybe,' I said.

Then Dad was hovering in the doorway as well. 'Your friends are welcome here any time, Marcus. But we did expressly ask you not to invite that girl . . .'

'I didn't invite *that girl*, as you keep calling her, although you know her name well enough. She just turned up with Joel. Now Tallulah – there, I've dared say her name aloud – has gone. And it's all over and done – sorted. OK?' I just wanted them both gone from my room now.

Dad did then lumber off, but Mum had to deliver one last parting shot. 'I hope Joel comes to his senses soon. I hear from his parents that his girlfriend is really lovely. As, of course, is your new girlfriend.'

After my parents had left, the peace was wonderful for five seconds. Then the guilt just flooded in.

How could I let Tallulah walk into danger on her own?

9.20 p.m.

But, blog, I didn't tell her to go to that stupid fair tonight. In fact, I tried to talk her out of it. She made that decision all by herself.

9.30 p.m.

She'll be at the fair now. At this very moment Tallulah could be confronting that phoney ventriloquist. Well, it's her choice.

9.31 p.m.

I've already been attacked by two deadly vampires. And a return match awaits me. I'd be insane to get involved in this too.

9.32 p.m.

Totally insane.

9.33 p.m.

But I can't not get involved either. Pacing about in my bedroom imagining what's happening to her is sheer torture.

9.34 p.m.

So yes, you guessed it. I am going to that wretched fair *again*. I don't want to.

But I just can't do anything else.

Only first I've got to get past my parents.

9.45 p.m.

I strolled up to Mum in the kitchen and said, 'You're right about Joel. He mustn't go out with Tallulah. So I'm going to warn him right now.'

Mum, who'd been clinking cutlery in the drawer, stopped and faced me. 'Can't you just call him?'

'No, no,' I said, already moving away further from her. 'This has to be done face to face. I'll tell him everything you said – and I won't be long.'

I was out of the front door before Mum could reply. She called something else after me about the snow. I didn't catch it, but I could guess. Fat, glittering snowflakes were tumbling everywhere. The first snow we'd seen all winter – always a great moment, even now. It really cheered me up as I half ran to the fair.

9.55 p.m.

No sign of the snowman tonight. No doubt

he'd turn up soon enough. But the only person I was looking for was Tallulah.

And then I saw her, standing outside the ventriloquist's tent, flakes of snow whirling around her. Had she been in the tent already? But then she saw me and said, 'I knew you'd come – in the end.'

'So you haven't gone in . . . ?'

'No, I was waiting for you. You took your time.'

'Well, I'm very sorry,' I said, grinning at her.

She moved forward. 'And, Marcus, I'll never tell about your relatives, not in the whole of my life—'

I stopped smiling and interrupted sharply, 'There's nothing to tell – it's just Cyril playing stupid games, which is all he's good for. And if you say one more thing about it I'm going right back home again.'

'All I seem to do tonight is apologize to you. But I am sorry – and the only important thing is that we're a team.'

'Yeah, it is,' I agreed. 'And you're the leader.'

'Of course I am,' she said, with a glint of a

smile. 'Actually, Marcus, I think this will be easy.'

If it was so easy I wondered why she hadn't just slipped in on her own.

Tallulah continued, 'We say "The game's up" to Rathbone. That's very important as he'll hate that. Then we go on and say stuff to really humiliate him.'

'After which he'll just conveniently vaporize away,' I said.

'Well, yes – Cyril said their pride is so powerful—'

'That's the Cyril who is now in hiding,' I interrupted.

'Well, yeah. OK, Cyril has gone all cowardly but that doesn't mean we have to as well. And I really think we can do this.' She was positively glowing with excitement and determination now. And it was kind of infectious.

'OK, let's do it before I come to my senses,' I said. Tallulah paid the boy hovering outside the tent. 'I hope we can claim all this money back on expenses,' I said.

And then we stepped inside.

CHAPTER TWENTY-ONE

Monday 5 January

10.15 p.m.

As before, the darkness inside the tent seemed to swallow everything up. But then we could make out dim shapes looming ahead of us.

'It's about time they started paying their electricity bills and put some lights on in here,' I said. Then I looked at Tallulah. 'Are you all right?' She seemed to be gasping for breath. 'Are you OK?' I asked again.

'Yeah, it's just Rathbone has really piled on the aftershave tonight.' And he had. Yet underneath that smell was a stale, rotting stench. Funny, I hadn't noticed it before. But not even Rathbone's gallons of aftershave could disguise it tonight – the stink of a vampire.

'I don't believe it. He's back again,' called Hugo.

'Oh, the surprises don't stop there, Hugo,' I snapped.

Tallulah and I barged past the little table where we'd sat before and marched right up to Rathbone who, as usual, had Hugo perched on his knee.

Hugo was screeching at us, 'You must sit down! Sit down now!'

'Sorry, Hugo, but it's Mr Rathbone we've come to talk to.'

'Mr Rathbone,' said Tallulah gravely, 'the game's up. We know who you really are. You're one of the so-called deadly vampires. The other is the snowman. You're the two people behind the Blood Ghost.'

I had to admire Rathbone's cool. Not so much as a twitch of apprehension. But it worried me too. Didn't animals stay completely still just before pouncing on their victim? Was that what he was about to do? Would he suddenly spring up and attack us?

Nervous but fired up as well, I joined in the attack. 'We've sussed out your whole plot, us lowly humans. Now there's nothing you can do. I won that fight with you two nights ago and now I've won again. Face it, Rathbone, you and that dead-behind-the-eyes snowman are two useless, pathetic deadly vampires.'

'You're totally finished,' cut in Tallulah. 'It's all over. The game's up.' She kept chanting those words as if they were part of a magic spell. 'So there's nothing for you to do now,' she went on, 'except leave here for good. So, bye-bye.' She started to laugh then, loudly, mockingly. And I joined in. Tallulah was right. She and I really were a good team. And we'd totally humiliated Rathbone.

Surely his pride couldn't take any more. But it seemed he could. He didn't say a word, just stayed eerily still. I even looked behind me in case the snowman had crept in behind us. But there was no one. Rathbone was acting as if we weren't there.

'Come on, put some lights on and talk to us properly,' I shouted. I darted forward and just tapped Rathbone lightly on the shoulder. That was all I did – honestly.

And that's when Rathbone did move.

He toppled forward and fell to the ground.

CHAPTER TWENTY-TWO

Monday 5 January

10.15 p.m. (cont'd)

I sprang back.

Had he had a stroke, or a heart attack? The shock of me ranting at him must have brought it on. Maybe he was a very ancient vampire. It was impossible to judge any vampire's age.

I turned to Tallulah. 'We'll have to get him help, won't we?'

To my total surprise she said, 'It's all right, I'll examine him.'

Before I could reply she'd walked forward and then bent down and lifted up Rathbone's head. She started to study him. I was amazed by her calmness.

'Is he still breathing?' I asked.

'No,' she said.

I gaped at her in horror.

'He never started,' she said. 'Look.'

I peered down at Rathbone's slumped body. Two glassy eyes stared back lifelessly at me. 'He's the dummy,' I cried, very relieved and very shocked at the same time.

Tallulah nodded grimly.

'No wonder they never let us see him properly. But if he's the dummy . . . ?' My question hung in the air for just a moment before Hugo leaped to his feet so swiftly and unexpectedly that Tallulah and I jumped away from him – and Rathbone.

'Look what you've done to him.' Hugo fired the words at us accusingly. 'Just leave him alone.' Then, gently, even tenderly, he lifted Mr Rathbone up and sat him on his chair once more. 'You're all right,' he murmured. 'Just had a bit of a fall, that's all.'

So Hugo – who could drain a human of blood without a moment's hesitation – could also lovingly nurse a block of wood.

Tallulah and I watched him, transfixed. For a moment Hugo seemed to have forgotten we were in the room. But then he started to square up to us. He was very small, about the size of a ten-year-old boy, but his face was pinched and wizened with huge, rage-filled eyes which I now recognized as belonging to the giant bat that had terrorized me. Hugo: an exceptionally small deadly vampire who could transform himself into the mightiest bat I'd ever seen. How he must love that.

He watched us with his feet planted apart and head forward, as if he were waiting to take part in a relay race.

'You're a disgrace to the good name of vampires,' Tallulah cried. 'You've nearly killed some humans.'

'You deadly vampires did kill a human once,' I said. 'A boy.'

'Humans leave the world so that something far more powerful and worthwhile can come into it. It sounds like a fair exchange to me.' His voice — and I assume this was his real voice now — was low and hoarse. But there was that preening confidence too, which made him so dislikeable. 'For centuries vampires have said this isn't our world any more.' He moved closer to us, giving us a strong whiff of his aftershave. 'So they've been content to skulk about in the shadows. But what kind of existence is that? Time for us to transform things,' he said.

'By attacking humans?' I said.

'We've barely started,' said Hugo.

'But the game's up,' shouted Tallulah.

'And we've rumbled you,' I added.

'So what?' snapped Hugo. 'Oh, sorry, I was forgetting. Aren't I supposed to be covered in confusion and shame and instantly disappear now? That's how the old vampires behaved. They make me ashamed. But it's different this time.'

'How?' I demanded.

'Because I'm not the only Blood Ghost vampire, as you humans call us here.'

'We know that,' said Tallulah. 'The snowman . . .'

Hugo threw back his head and gave a laugh, which was more of a howl. 'I knew you'd think that,' he said gleefully.

'So the snowman isn't a vampire,' cried Tallulah disbelievingly.

'Oh, yes he is, and with a deep hatred of traitors' – Hugo flashed a glance at me – 'who he can spot instantly. But he's not a *deadly* vampire; he's not part of our campaign. And while you've been distracted by him, other vampires, who have learned the benefits of huge quantities of human blood, have been arriving. They're here now. That's why I shan't extinguish with shame, as you were no doubt expecting.' Hugo moved forward. 'And let me tell you, the Blood Ghost was just the start. In Great Walden tomorrow comes the first mass demonstration of our power. Something which will send humans rocking back on their heels.'

As he spoke now he seemed to expand with confidence. Small as he was, he seemed to fill the room with his dark scheme.

'But what exactly are you going to do?' demanded Tallulah.

'You will have to be just a little more patient,' said Hugo with a nauseating little grin. 'For now I'd be more concerned about your own personal safety.'

'You've had two goes at me already,' I said.

'And I could so easily finish you off right now. But no, I shall make you wait a little longer. I can promise you a third meeting very, very soon though. And don't forget, we are not limited to the night. We can strike at any time. So you'd better run off home while you can.'

'We will stop you somehow,' said Tallulah.

'No one can stop us this time,' Hugo said. 'And certainly not you two,' he called after us in a voice full of contempt.

As we left the tent we saw a couple waiting to go in. 'I wouldn't bother,' I said to them, 'as the dummy's a real person. Tell all your friends.'

Then Tallulah whispered to me, 'Do you think Hugo was bluffing?'

'No.'

'Neither do I. We haven't stopped him at all.'

'Well, we didn't know all the facts. Like there are more of them here already.'

'Shall I text Cyril the news?' she asked.

'Yeah, and if he can be bothered to drop by before it all kicks off tomorrow, that would be super.'

CHAPTER TWENTY-THREE

Monday 5 January

10.20 p.m.

I insisted on seeing Tallulah home.

'There's no need,' she said grumpily.

'I know,' I said, walking beside her. 'By the way, when exactly are you off to the sanatorium?'

'There's a nice, cheerful question.'

'What's the answer?'

She sighed. 'Oh, very soon. Next week, I think. But I'll probably run away first. And can we change the subject now?'

'We can't, actually.' I swallowed and then said, 'Tallulah, what bug have you got?'

'Don't worry, it's not infectious,' she snapped.

183

I flinched. 'Sometimes you can be the most annoying person in the world.'

'Only sometimes?'

'No, just about every second, actually. Look, I couldn't care less about it being infectious, as you well know. I just wanted to know what it is.'

'No one knows,' said Tallulah.

'No one,' I echoed.

'It's a total mystery as the doctors can't identify my bug, and if they can't identify it they can't treat it either. So now I'm being shipped off to a sanatorium, where all these doctors will do zillions and zillions of tests on me to try and find out my bug's sensitivity, and I can't tell you how I'm dreading it and I *hate*' – she shouted this last word at me – 'even talking about it.' Then she walked away from me at such a fast pace I had to half run to keep up with her.

'Tallulah—' I began.

'No,' she cried. 'Not another word about—'

'I just wanted to say thanks for telling me.'

'OK.' She stopped and looked at me. She even smiled very briefly and then said, 'And

184

now can we talk about far more important stuff like deadly vampires.'

'Yeah, we can,' I said. 'Now, before it all kicks off in Great Walden, Hugo and his chums are going to try and deal with us, and they can strike at any time now – maybe even on the way to school. So I think you should stay in all day tomorrow.'

'I will,' she said slowly, 'if you do too.'

'I won't even leave to make a snowman.'

She actually laughed at that, and when we'd reached her house she said, 'Look after yourself, Marcus.' And she sounded as if she really meant that too.

'You too.'

I felt as if I should say something else, but my mind had gone blank. I started to trudge away. Then I looked back. She was still standing outside.

'What are you doing?' I asked.

'I'll go in when I'm ready,' she replied. 'Right now I'm watching it snowing.'

But actually I think she was summoning up the courage to face her family. Poor Tallulah. I wanted to speed back and give her a hug. But I didn't. Instead, I decided I'd better go home. So I took a short cut through a laneway near her house. It was very narrow – more like a tunnel really – and very dark, save for the snow which was really pelting down now.

As I came out of the laneway I passed a man out with his dog. 'It's settling,' he announced.

'Great,' I said.

'And it's getting slippery already,' he said.

Everything was so normal and everyday one moment. And the next I heard a sound that made my scalp tighten with shock and fear.

Someone was yelling for help.

And I recognized the voice instantly. Well, I should have done.

It was me.

Or rather it was someone impersonating me.

Why? It didn't make any sense.

And then, with a terrible thud of horror, it did.

CHAPTER TWENTY-FOUR

Tuesday 6 January

6.25 a.m.

I've just woken up.

Outside, no birds are chattering. No one even drives past. Total silence. Normally I like the way snow smothers every single noise. But not today.

It unnerves me.

And then I gaze around my bedroom. There in the corner are my two bags all packed. Very soon, I'll be far away from here. I haven't a clue when I'll return.

Yet I feel oddly calm about that. It seems almost unimportant compared to all the other things that have happened. So much stuff to tell you and I don't want to tell you about any of it. Writing it down makes it too real.

What a total, total nightmare these last hours have been. But somehow I've got to try and make sense of it. So I'll take you back to when I heard someone calling for help and impersonating my voice. The shock of that made me giddy for a moment.

Then I knew with total certainty that it was a trap – for Tallulah.

One of the deadly vampires – probably Hugo – was pretending to be me, calling for help. Of course, Tallulah would race to my rescue and straight into an ambush.

As I pelted back I knew exactly where the ambush would be too – down that dark, deserted laneway.

I'll never forget what I saw next – Tallulah fighting off what looked like a thick, black cloud. There weren't just one or even two giant bats swooping and whirling at her. No, there were five of them. She'd push one away and another would instantly rise up.

I ran towards Tallulah so fast I stumbled. And I half fell into the line of battle, not thinking at all about what I was doing. There wasn't time to feel scared or brave. I just charged at those bats like a mad bull.

And they totally ignored me. They just went on flapping and diving at Tallulah, until suddenly she gave a tiny scream. It sounded more like a frightened puppy than Tallulah.

And then Tallulah was lying on the snow.

Instantly all those bats rose up into the air like a terrible plume of dark smoke, sending a whiff of mould and decay flying everywhere. And then they vanished. They were like a flock of assassins who, the moment they'd performed their hit, knew their work was done and were gone.

I tore forward. I picked Tallulah up in my arms and nearly asked her, 'Are you all right?' The stupidest question in the history of stupid questions. But instead, she tried to say something to me. She opened her mouth, her hands started to shake, but no words came. Then she gave a little sigh.

It was icy cold now, so I tore off my coat and put it round her. And I had to get her help. Should I ring for an ambulance, or take her back to her house? I'd do both. I fumbled for my phone and by its light saw on her neck a tiny bite mark.

Most humans would have missed it, thinking it was only a sting of some sort. It was so small. But I knew it was the mark of the vampire. I'd seen exactly the same marks on Marilyn's neck after the Blood Ghost had attacked her.

Only Tallulah didn't just have one of the bites. There were five of them.

It was a massacre.

The next moment I felt a hand on my shoulder. I whirled round. And there, weirdly, unbelievably, were my parents. I gaped at them. 'You were gone so long,' began Mum, 'that we came looking for you.'

And what had happened to Tallulah was so terrible that the strangeness of them suddenly appearing like that just melted away. I struggled to speak. 'Tallulah . . . attack . . . vampire bats.'

I'd said the V word in public, but for once my parents didn't tell me off. All the normal rules were suspended.

And Mum, who just hours earlier had been rubbishing Tallulah, now said, 'The poor child,' with such sadness and pain in her voice.

Dad very carefully took Tallulah from me. She was lying very still now.

'I was – to ring—' I still couldn't talk in proper sentences. 'Get ambulance . . .'

But then Dad looked up and said slowly, 'I don't think there's much hope for her.'

CHAPTER TWENTY-FIVE

Tuesday 6 January

6.25 a.m. (cont'd)

Tears started rolling down my face. And my voice was thick and muffled as I shouted. 'No, we've got . . . do something. Must save her!'

Mum touched my arm and said very quietly to Dad. 'Hold her steady,' as she bent over Tallulah's neck. She looked – well, just like a vampire. I even felt myself shudder.

'What are you doing to her?' I demanded.

'Trying to save her life,' said Dad. 'What do you think?' He went on, 'But this will only work if we' – and by *we* he meant half-vampires – 'get there very quickly after the attack. And not many of us can do it.'

'Do what?' I asked, as Mum continued to loom menacingly over Tallulah.

Dad said softly, 'There are so many bites on Tallulah's neck that it's triggering a very severe reaction. But your mum's saliva contains an antidote which will lessen the effect – and then . . .' He paused.

'Then what?'

'Well, then Tallulah's got half a chance.'

Mum paused and muttered something to Dad.

'What did Mum say?' I asked.

'There are five bites,' said Dad.

'I know that.'

'But she's concentrating on the two main ones. These are the ones which are causing such a strong reaction. Now you keep watch, Marcus.'

I totally understood we didn't want any humans seeing what Mum was doing. They'd never understand. Dad went on, 'And ring for an ambulance. I just hope it can get through. Some of the main roads are blocked already. Give them Tallulah's address very clearly. We'll take her there when your mum has finished.'

I did that, while keeping a look-out for anyone walking down the laneway. But no one came by – the deadly vampires had chosen their location well.

Mum finished all her emergency first aid and said Tallulah was showing some signs of responding. I kept staring at Tallulah, willing her to open her eyes or something. But she just lay there with flakes of snow settling all over her. Mum said it was too early for any positive reaction yet, and I mustn't get my hopes up as the vampire attack had been the most severe she'd ever seen.

Then Dad carried Tallulah to her house. 'Oh no, no,' wailed her mum when she saw her. 'I told her not to go out tonight. Where did you find her?' Soon Tallulah's whole family were clambering round her while I said how we'd been walking back from the fair when she'd just collapsed. And when I was trying to help her my mum and dad had turned up.

'Stupid, stupid girl,' said Tallulah's dad. 'But you can't tell her anything. No one can. She's at war with the world.' He carried her over to the fire.

'Oh, where's that ambulance?' wailed her mum.

It took much longer than usual. In fact, there were delays everywhere because of the snow. But finally, finally it appeared, and about half of Tallulah's neighbours in her road came out or peeked through their windows.

'Did she fall in the snow?' one neighbour asked. If only it had been as simple as that.

I was nervy and sick and scared and ashamed and lonely all at once. And I'd never felt more tired in my life. It was as if a great weight had rolled right onto me. I was very worried about Tallulah. But I also knew my life would never be the same again. The consequences of what had happened tonight would be with me for a very long time.

Finally Tallulah's mum and dad left in the ambulance with her. My parents offered to stay behind to look after the other children, but a neighbour had turned up, so then we trudged back home.

The shocking turn of events had temporarily wiped out everything. But as we walked very slowly down the road, Mum told how they'd come looking for me, worried about all the snow forecasts. I guessed that wasn't the only reason. They were very concerned about Tallulah turning up tonight too.

They'd gone to Joel's house first. Then, finding no sign of me – or Tallulah – they decided to try Tallulah's house. They weren't quite sure where her road was. And while walking about they'd found us both.

'I'm so glad you did,' I said.

And I really was.

Without my mum, Tallulah wouldn't have had a chance.

But I knew a big interrogation was on its way now.

6.31 a.m.

It came after we'd rung up Tallulah's parents at the hospital to find out how she was. They said she was being carefully monitored in the intensive care unit and everything possible was being done. So they didn't tell us anything really. But Mum said Tallulah had a chance – a good chance, she thought.

And then came the moment when I had to tell my parents what had really been happening since New Year's Day (which seems light years away already).

I didn't want to lie any more. Well, I couldn't. I was too tired for a start (lying uses up incredible energy) and I suppose I felt I owed it to my parents to come clean.

So the only thing I missed out was Cyril wondering if I had half-vampire connections. My parents had enough to worry about without burdening them with that news too. Of course, I also didn't tell them about Tallulah overhearing Cyril and me talking.

But I recounted everything else, including Tallulah and me being enlisted as vampire fighters by Cyril. And when I related how we'd gone to the fair to track down the deadly vampire, Mum's mouth just fell open. She was beyond horrified, while Dad's head fell so low I thought it was going to crash onto the table any minute.

But they didn't interrupt me. The only other sound was the wind whistling and sighing away outside whilst pelting still more snow against the window. Actually, I think the weather made my exploits sound even worse than they were.

But they were pretty bad, I totally admit that. And when I'd finished I said as cheerfully as I could, 'And that's all, so please feel free now to ask questions, pass out or hit me with a baseball bat.'

There was an awful heavy silence while the horror at what I'd done just grew and grew. I could almost see it, looming over everything else. Finally Mum murmured, 'I just can't believe . . .' And then her voice drifted away again.

Finally Dad slowly raised his head. 'So all the time we thought you were worrying about your special power, you were really thinking about fighting vampires.'

'I was concerned about my special power too.'

'Oh, were you?' snapped Dad, so sharply it was like the crack of a whip. 'You stupid boy. Do you have any idea what you've done?' Dad never raised his voice – not even now – but somehow the walls still shook with his anger. 'You're totally to blame for what happened to that girl tonight. She was just a silly, deluded thrill-seeker. But you – you should have known better. You *do*

198

know better. So why didn't you stop her?'

'I couldn't, because—'

'You didn't even try,' said Dad. 'You were just showing off, encouraging her—'

'No, I wasn't doing that,' I interrupted. 'I was—'

'We've heard enough from you,' snapped Dad. 'Your mother and I only asked you to do two things. Stay away from Tallulah – and vampires. That's all you had to do. And we asked you to do that for our own safety and yours. But instead you—'

'I'm sorry, Dad.'

'No, don't you dare say that when you don't mean it,' snapped Dad. He was up from his seat and circling round me now. 'For you'd do it all again, wouldn't you? At least be honest.'

'No, I wouldn't,' I began. 'But—'

'But . . . ?' Dad pounced on the word.

I stared miserably at him and Mum – who still seemed to be in a state of total shock. 'Those deadly vampires have got to be stopped,' I said quietly.

'But not by us,' said Dad. 'We're no match for them. Well, you saw what they did to that girl tonight. And now you've brought the most treacherous vampires of all right to our door.'

'No—' I began.

'Oh, yes you have. Normally they leave us alone and we leave them alone, but you've interfered and inflamed them so much you've made yourself their number one target. And you've put not only your own life in serious jeopardy but your mother's and mine too.'

'Oh, he doesn't care about that,' said Mum, speaking for the first time. 'What happens to us is of no concern to him at all.'

'That's not true!' I practically shouted. 'I really didn't want all this to kick off. And whatever you want me to do I'll do.'

'All right,' said Dad. 'Go upstairs and pack a bag.'

Even Mum looked stunned by this. For a mad moment I actually thought he was chucking me out. But then Dad went on, 'It's too dangerous to stay here. We'll all have to leave.'

'Where to?' asked Mum.

'I don't know yet,' said Dad. 'I'll have to make some phone calls. And you'—he pointed at me – 'don't come down here again until it's time to leave. I can't even bear to look at you right now.'

Upstairs I thought I'd explode with shame. I kept seeing myself through my parents' eyes. The son who'd let them down yet again. There they were, eagerly awaiting news of my special power, which never came. And instead they were going to have to flee their home because I'd got myself mixed up with the most dangerous vampires around.

The pain and frustration inside me kept twisting about until I couldn't bear it. I had to do something, so I called Gracie.

'Hey, what about all this snow, then,' she began, but quickly sensed something was wrong. 'Come on, tell me what's happened. It can't be that bad.'

'You wait,' I said.

When I told her about Tallulah she was really shocked. 'But still,' she went on, 'going off and tackling those deadly vampires. You were both incredibly brave.'

'That's not how my parents see it.' I recounted some of their comments.

'But if you'd turned your back on Tallulah she'd be in a terrible mess.'

'She's in a pretty bad way now.'

'But you helped her when you really didn't want to. I call that being a true friend.'

'Tell my mum and dad that.'

'I will, if you want me to.'

I smiled for the first time in what felt like centuries. 'You sound really mad now.'

'I am, actually. That's the trouble with your parents and my mum, they don't want to hear our point of view. They're always right and no one else's opinions matter. Especially ours.'

'I'm so glad I rang you,' I said.

'So ring me any time. I'm doing absolutely nothing except getting more hairy.' Then she added anxiously, 'But don't try and be a superhero again, will you?'

Later Mum came upstairs and brought me some beetroot sandwiches. 'Hey, Mum, thanks, this is great,' I said, acting a bit over-enthusiastically because I thought it was a peace offering.

But actually I don't think it was, as she just announced grimly, 'They've said on the radio that all the roads – even the main ones – are impassable tonight. So your father thinks it's best if we wait until morning, when the snow should have stopped, and just barricade ourselves in here for now. Keep every window in here tightly closed, all right?'

Before I could reply, Mum had gone. She didn't say anything about me coming back downstairs either. So I stayed in my bedroom.

Then, about half past four, I went to the bathroom. On the way I bumped into my dad. He was standing right outside my bedroom like my own private sentry.

I tried to talk to him, but he just shook his head at me. He was still furious with me – yet he was also standing guard over me. Actually, I think he was outside my bedroom most of the night.

Now he's gone.

And I've just heard someone go downstairs. I'm not sure if it's him or Mum. But we'll be on the move very soon. Haven't a clue where I'll be writing my next blog from.

CHAPTER TWENTY-SIX

Tuesday 6 January

7.40 a.m.

We haven't left yet.

All the bags are piled up downstairs.

But the local radio said most of the main roads are still impassable. And the police are advising everyone to stay at home unless their journeys are 'very urgent'.

'Well, our journey *is* very urgent,' Dad said to Mum. 'But we can give it another couple of hours or so.'

'Where exactly are we going?' I asked.

'We'll tell you when you need to know,' snapped Dad.

I'd never known him as angry as this for

so long before. I was really in disgrace this time. The radio announcer also read out a list of schools which were closed for the day. Just about every school, it seemed, including mine.

Normally Joel and I would be off now looking for someone to have a massive snowball fight with. No chance of that today.

7.55 a.m.

Dad let me ring up the hospital. But the hospital wouldn't tell us anything since we weren't relatives.

I wanted to ring Tallulah's parents again to find out more. Dad said they'd call us when they had news, but right now I must leave them in peace. It was the longest conversation he had with me this morning. Breakfast was especially grim.

Mum and Dad answered each one of my questions with one- or two-word answers. It was as if talking to me at all required superhuman effort.

9.50 a.m.

Something weird.

I was thinking about Gracie, wondering if I should ring her now or wait until later. She might still be having her breakfast. I'd just decided I'd wait when Gracie called me.

'It's OK,' she said. 'I had my breakfast yonks ago.'

It turned out she'd picked up my voice – but coming and going. She couldn't catch everything, but heard something about me wondering if she'd had her breakfast.

Once before, when I had a kind of preview of my special power, I'd sent Gracie an urgent message through telepathy. Incredibly useful it had been, too. Was it happening again now?

We both became really excited then – until I tried to send Gracie another message: just something about how deep the snow was. But she never received it.

'Your special power is still trying to break through,' said Gracie.

'Or maybe I've just got a very faulty special power,' I said.

'Don't be like that.' Gracie half laughed. 'Are your hands tingling at all?'

'Not really,' I said.

'Well, they will do soon.' Gracie sounded very confident.

But I didn't say anything to my parents. Better to wait until I know something definite.

10.05 a.m.

Dad's put all our cases in the car now. I'm still not even sure where we're going. He just said something about a trusted contact.

10.20 a.m.

I was waiting upstairs in my bedroom, trying to relax with a favourite computer game. So I didn't notice the air shift slightly. And I didn't glimpse a figure slowly materializing in the corner of my room.

Not until he called out my name.

I turned round.

And there he was.

Colin.

CHAPTER TWENTY-SEVEN

Tuesday 6 January

10.20 a.m.

This time I'd have known Colin was a ghost right away.

He was slightly blurred and out of focus for a start. And he looked as pale as a ... well, ghost. Just looking at him made me feel as if I were half in a dream. And I felt, well, not exactly nervous of him ... but he was someone who wasn't alive. And that was pretty eerie – at first.

But then he grinned so triumphantly and looked so chuffed to see me that I quickly forgot all that and just thought, *Brilliant, my mate is back.*

Colin said, 'I can't believe I'm here. Can't tell you how hard it was getting through again.'

'Can anyone else see you?' I asked.

'Not sure. Maybe. Haven't a clue, actually. I just concentrated on you seeing me again.'

'The last time,' I said, 'I had no idea you were a . . .'

'A half-vampire.' Colin sort of whistled the word.

'I was going to say a ghost.'

'Well, I'm both of those.' Colin said this almost shyly. But then he gazed outside. 'Hey, will you look at all this snow?'

'You like snow, then?' I asked.

'Oh yeah, especially when it's a big surprise,' said Colin. 'You wake up and notice your curtains are glowing slightly. Then you pull them back and there's all this snow just waiting for you.'

He stared outside longingly for a moment and then kind of shook himself. 'Marcus, I don't know how long you'll be able to see me, so I've got to talk fast – and warn you about these new deadly vampires.'

'Too late,' I said. 'I know I should have

stayed away from them, but I didn't and my parents said I've been very stupid—'

'But it wouldn't have mattered if you'd found them or not,' interrupted Colin excitedly. 'They'd still have come looking for you. Just like they did me.'

I stared at him. 'But why?'

'Because I'm a half-vampire' – again he sort of whistled this – 'with a special power. And so are you, aren't you?'

'Yeah,' I began, and then I shook my head. 'But I don't have my special power yet – and anyway, why would it bother these vampires?'

'Because we haven't just got one special power, we've got tons of them. That's why we're known as a one-in-a-thousand half-vampire.'

'A what?' I said, so shocked I plonked myself down on my bed.

'A one-in-a-thousand half-vampire. They're the really special ones – mega-strong and good at fighting—'

'And I'm one?' I interrupted, my heart beating like a thousand hammers.

'That's right.'

But that was impossible. I mean, it was pushing it for me to have one special power, let alone . . . Then I saw Colin was laughing.

'What?'

'You look as if your face is about to fall off.'

'Well, I can't believe it – me!'

Colin said. 'That's why you're a prime target. Vampires can sense if half-vampires are going to have all these special powers which even overtake their own. Of course they hate it. And this mad gang know we can stop them. That's why, nine years ago, they came looking for me. They got me too, before my special powers had come through.'

'And now they want to do the same with me,' I said.

'That's right.'

'But my parents never said anything about me being—'

'They don't know. Only vampires can pick it up, like a scent off you. They'll come for you again, Marcus. But if your special power comes through first, they won't stand a chance. You can see them off. And when you're fighting them, Marcus, fight them for me too.'

'But I'm normally the world's worst fighter.

Teddy bears pick fights with me. And without those special powers—'

Then I stopped as Colin was starting to fade away. 'Hey, not already,' he groaned.

'Come back later,' I said.

'Can't,' said Colin. 'I really think this is it. We shan't meet again.' Then his face disappeared completely.

But then, like an echo from somewhere far away, I heard him cry, *'The power is there inside you, Marcus – just waiting to break out.'*

CHAPTER TWENTY-EIGHT

Tuesday 6 January

10.45 a.m.

'I AM' – I yelled silently – 'A ONE-IN-A-THOUSAND HALF-VAMPIRE.'

I'm literally magic.

No wonder I can't get my head around it. It still seems totally impossible. So I'm excited but baffled. *Me*, of all people.

And that explains why I was top of the deadly vampires' hit list. Nothing to do with me going to the fair. No, they'd already targeted me. And next time they'll really want to finish me off. And if my special powers don't come through, they'll do it too – with ease.

Yet the last thing Colin said was that the

power was there inside me now, waiting to break out.

So I've just got to release it.

Just!

And what's stopping it anyway? Is it me? What did Tara say? 'You've built up an invisible wall.'

Time to smash that wall down – and fast!

11.25 a.m.

I was trying to do those exercises Tara taught me. You know, all that shaking hands with my half-vampire self. I just felt stupid, though. Tara was supposed to be coming round tonight, but that would be too late. So could I ask her to coach me down the phone? I was about to do just that when it happened again! Tara rang me, saying that my voice kept floating in and out of her head asking for help.

So every so often my special power (or one of them!) is spluttering into life. This encouraged me. Then I asked Tara for some tips.

'Just open yourself up,' she said.

'You say that, but what exactly does it mean?' I asked.

'Right, do this exercise with me right now,' she said. 'Sense your special power now; smell it, believe in it, let it flood you.' She burbled on like this for ages. And to be honest it wasn't really helping. I think she sensed this, for she suddenly said, 'The only barrier is you.'

'I don't get that,' I said.

'You're still fighting your special power.'

'I really am not.'

'Yes, you are, because if you had one wish which could come true now, it wouldn't be to bring out your special power. No, your biggest dream is still to be normal. I'm right, aren't I?'

The question took me totally by surprise. 'Well, possibly . . .' I began.

'The truth is,' said Tara, 'being normal is one choice you just don't have – and never will again. You're weird for ever. Deal with it.'

'Don't mince your words, will you,' I muttered.

'But here's the thing, Marcus,' she practically shouted. 'Weird is bold, exciting and adventurous and I'd choose it over grey, boring, tedious, normal any day. You're really very lucky, only you just won't see it. Start seeing it.'

'OK, I will,' I promised.

'And put your whole self into seeing it, because if you don't, your special power will just wither away ... taking a big chunk of you along with it.'

'I totally get everything you're saying,' I said. 'But just one last question: what's a one-in-a-thousand half-vampire?'

'Ah, you've heard about them, have you? Well, a very tiny number of half-vampires don't just have one power, they have a whole multitude of them. It's very, very rare, though. Still, nothing like being ambitious. That's the spirit.'

11.55 a.m.

I was madly shaking hands with my half-vampire self (in fact my right hand has got cramp now) when Joel rang. He started to tell me about a massive snowball fight planned for five thirty today. 'It's going to be like the Battle of Waterloo – only better.'

I'd love to have been in on that, but instead I had to tell Joel I'd had a big row with my parents and wasn't allowed out right now (and I couldn't tell him that in fact I'd probably be miles away from here by half past five. Dad's scraping the snow off the drive right now and refusing any help from me).

Joel groaned. 'When your parents called round my house looking for you and Tallulah I thought you might be in trouble.'

'Actually,' I said, 'Tallulah's in hospital right now.'

Joel was totally stunned by that news. 'What happened to her?'

Just remembering what did happen made my voice shake a bit. 'She was out in the snow when she collapsed.'

'She's been sort of ill for yonks, hasn't she?'

I agreed she had.

'But she was so different round your home last night, almost nice. Poor old Tallulah. Still, she'll be out soon. And when you speak to her, say hi from me. It'll probably give her a relapse. But say I wish her all the best.'

And as I thought of Tallulah stuck in that hospital, I felt this great roar of anger explode inside me. Those deadly vampires had to be stopped! And if I was the one person who could do it – then I was definitely up for that.

So now it's back to shaking hands with my half-vampire self.

12.05 p.m.

Just a few minutes ago Mum and I were waiting outside with our bags, while all the time looking round more than a bit fearfully. Meanwhile Dad had gone into the garage to get the car out. Soon we would speed away to a secret location.

Only it didn't quite happen like that. Instead, the car spluttered into life for eight seconds and promptly died again. Dad hasn't been able to start it up since. So now he's rung up the local garage. If they can get through, someone will come over later this afternoon. Until then we're stuck here.

'We should be safe until then,' said Dad.

'Yes,' agreed Mum. 'It's at night they'll try . . .' Then her voice fell away.

No one asked my opinion. But I wasn't so sure. The deadly vampires could strike at any time. So would they really wait until night time? I was absolutely certain they'd deal with me before that. Still, every door and window is firmly locked. There's no way they can get in.

12.45 p.m.

The doorbell's just rung twice and very loudly (or so it seemed), making all three of us jump.

'No one answers the door – except me,' said Dad. Then he called out, 'Er – who is it?'

One of our neighbours, Mrs Rogers, called back. Dad slid back the bolts on the front door.

Mrs Rogers said that none of the local shops had opened yet because of the snow, and she'd run out of milk and eggs. She's a total scrounger, actually, but Mum and Dad gave her tons of stuff. I think they were so relieved it was just her. And for a few minutes at least, everything here seemed reassuringly normal.

2.15 p.m.

I have good news. All my handshaking is starting to work. I can now feel a definite tingling in both my hands – the first sign that things are happening. And that wall is about to come tumbling down.

I decided to tell my mum and dad. I think with everything else going on they'd temporarily forgotten about my special power. But their faces instantly lit up when they heard.

And Dad touched me lightly on the arm. 'If we can just get through these next few hours, I know everything's going to be all right.' It was like my friendly old dad was back. I'd missed him.

And then the doorbell rang again.

We were a bit calmer this time. Dad just walked briskly to the front door and asked, 'Who is it?'

Back came a reply I'd never, ever expected. 'It's Cyril. We haven't actually met, but I know your son, Marcus. And now I need to talk to you urgently.'

'Did you invite him here?' demanded Mum of me at once.

'I didn't even give him my address,' I said.

'Well, he's found us anyway,' said Dad grimly. 'This foolish man who meddles with vampires and encourages you to do likewise is at our door.' Both Dad and Mum were looking at me very suspiciously now.

'Honestly, I never have asked him here. Cross my fangs.'

Dad looked at me, nodded and said quietly, 'Marcus, please go upstairs to your bedroom now. Close your door and you're not to come downstairs until I tell you. On no account are you to talk to this man.'

'That's fine with me.'

Dad waited for me to go upstairs and click my bedroom door shut before calling to Cyril, 'We shan't be a moment.'

I opened my door a crack. I could hear Dad unlocking the bolts again. Then I heard Cyril say, 'I'm so sorry to bother you, but it is vitally important.'

'Of course,' replied Dad smoothly. 'Please come in for a moment.' Then he introduced Mum, after which they were all talking so softly I couldn't hear a word. What was Cyril telling them? Was he about to get me in even more trouble with my parents? (Could I *be* in any more trouble?)

And why was he wasting his time dropping round here anyway? He should be tackling these deadly vampires. He knows who they are and where they hang out. All his delaying was just making everything worse.

2.20 p.m.

I've just been asked to come downstairs. Only not by Mum or Dad – but Cyril. 'We need to talk to you urgently, Marcus.' That's all he said. But there was something strange about his voice.

That's why I called back, 'Where's my dad?'

'Waiting downstairs for you,' said Cyril. 'So hurry up – all will be explained then.'

Something was wrong here all right. Dad would never have let Cyril talk for him. But I had to go downstairs to find out what was going on.

Back soon, blog, I hope.

CHAPTER TWENTY-NINE

Tuesday 6 January

6.05 p.m.

At last I can tell you what happened next.

I knew something was badly wrong as I pelted down the stairs. And I was actually relieved to find my parents standing together in the hallway.

'What does Cyril want?' I asked them. 'And where is he?'

Neither of my parents answered. Dad just stood there with one hand frozen in the air, as if he were playing statues. A terrible choking fear grew in me.

'Hey, Dad,' I croaked.

Dad struggled to speak and his lips moved

but no words came. All he could do was roll his eyes at me desperately and breathe in low, heavy gasps.

Mum, right beside him, had her head hanging down and a dazed look in her eyes. She struggled to talk as well, but with no more success than Dad.

Seeing them like that – my heart just stopped while tears rolled down my face. Rage flowed through me too. Why had Cyril done this to my parents? And how had he done it? Then, behind me, I heard Cyril say, 'There shouldn't be any lasting effects. They'll recover eventually – if you're sensible.'

I tore round to see . . . not Cyril at all, but Hugo in a brown cap, a very expensive-looking cape and huge boots, positively gloating at his own cleverness.

'How did you get in?' I began. But before I'd asked the question I knew the answer. 'You impersonated Cyril's voice,' I said.

'Such a useful talent,' said Hugo gleefully, then he bounded halfway up the stairs so he could loom over me. 'Very amusingly, Cyril really *was* coming here, to warn you about my forthcoming visit.' Hugo gave a laugh which was more like a sharp bark. 'Only we got to him first. So when I arrived here I impersonated his voice. I have such a talent for that. It was an extra piece of luck, of course, that you were upstairs when I called. And both your unsuspecting parents looked straight into my eyes and allowed me to hypnotize them so easily. But then you are rather elementary creatures, aren't you?'

He said this while half skipping about on the stairs, then he leaped down. 'Now I have no more interest in your parents. It is only you who can stop our plans coming to fruition, so I think it might be best if you and I leave them.'

I looked around wildly. I had to get out of here, get help for my parents. As if reading my thoughts, Hugo said, 'Your parents are beyond any human' – he spat that word at me – 'help. And I'd so hate them to feel even more uncomfortable.' Then he pointed a stumpy finger at me. 'But I certainly can do that.'

My dad raised a shaking finger like some ancient zombie. He was doing his best to show his huge anger with Hugo.

'Don't worry, Dad,' I whispered while more tears spilled down my face. 'I'll sort this.'

I had to think fast. Do something.

But what?

Well, I was now able to transmit messages, for some of the time at least. So should I try and contact Gracie? Get her to send help just as she'd done once before. But any help that arrived would come far too late. And who could help us anyway?

'Shall we adjourn to the sitting room?' said Hugo. 'After you,' he said. So I walked first, with Hugo following right behind me as if he were brandishing an invisible gun in his hand. Then I turned and faced Hugo. He only reached just above my shoulder. But his confidence radiated over everything. 'Don't worry,' he said. 'I'm a very sporting chap, so I shall give you a warning before the attack starts.'

'You spoil me,' I muttered.

Hugo surveyed my sitting room for a moment, and then plonked himself down on the sofa and looked so shockingly at ease it was as if he was granting me an audience in my own house.

And he didn't so much speak as purr.

'Well, to business. We shall have to deal with you very severely, I'm afraid. But we have no choice. You are in the way. And world-shattering events are about to happen here in Great Walden.'

'You mean you're going to terrorize more innocent people—'

'No human is innocent,' interrupted Hugo, his voice suddenly throbbing with hatred. 'They've kept us down, made us hide away and humiliated us.'

'That's rubbish. Most humans don't even know you exist,' I began.

Hugo got up and bounced towards me like some over-eager, monstrous child. 'Oh, but that will soon change. We shall shake up humans' lives all right, just as we shook up your girlfriend's – or one of them – last night.'

'Proud of that, are you? Proud that there's a girl in hospital, fighting for her life because of you.'

'Oh, very proud.' Then he let out a high-pitched giggle. A sound which made you never want to laugh again. And it was that revelling in his own nastiness which made my mind turn red. I so wanted to punch that twisted, smirking face, but instead I spat at him twice. Both pieces of gob landed right on his nose too – *splat!* He sprang back from me and he looked so shocked I even managed a small laugh.

'That's for Tallulah and my mum and dad,' I shouted.

Hugo wiped his nose in one furious movement, using the sleeve of his cape. He was livid, but he quickly recovered. 'How impolite, especially as we are, to coin an ancient cliché, not alone.'

'No one else has got in here,' I said at once.

Hugo raised an amused eyebrow. 'Now, I'm an old-school vampire. I like to be invited inside someone's house. But others today are far less refined, I regret to say, and don't care about such social etiquette any more. They just barge their way in.'

It was then I heard this scuffling noise from the fireplace, as if a bird was down there or a . . .

Out of a small explosion of coal dust emerged – a bat.

'No locks or bolts can keep us out,' said Hugo proudly, while the bat began to grow, transforming itself into a massive creature. It skimmed and skittered around the room – very leisurely and relaxed. Seemingly as confident here as Hugo.

But then its wings began to flutter like someone revving up a motorbike before charging into action. 'My friend is getting very impatient,' said Hugo. 'And so am I. You have other guests arriving here too.'

And right then I could hear more scuffling noises from the fireplace.

'But first, I cannot let your display of appalling manners go unpunished.' And the next thing I knew a great jagged bolt of lightning seemed to just fly off Hugo's finger – and straight into my face.

There was no time to duck away. I got it full force. And the red-hot pain was immediate and excruciating as it seared right through me. I remember once burning my hand and that was agonizing. But this felt as if I'd burned my whole body.

I shut my eyes as the pain continued to slice through me. And I heard Hugo exclaim,

'First time I've ever tried that, and what an amazing result!' Then he laughed and clapped his hands together.

That was the very last sound I heard before something dived right at me. Not one bat, but a whole squad of them. I couldn't even tell you how many. All I could see was this terrible whirring blur descending on me, while their smell hit me like a fist. It was like having twenty stink bombs hurled into my face at once.

The air was knocked out of my lungs and I was gagging and gasping for breath when the bats attacked. So I was stunned already. And before I knew what was going on sharp teeth started sliding down my neck. This was followed by such agonizing pain I yelled out and toppled over onto the floor.

And then everything was just a distorted mass of wings and foul smells, all diving right at me. They'd only been here a minute and already I was overpowered and about to pass out.

I couldn't fight them any more. I had no energy left for a start. A feeling of total hopelessness swept right through me then. So

Colin's fate was about to envelop me too. I didn't have any more of a chance than he did, despite all his efforts.

I should have known my special powers wouldn't turn up in time. Everything I touch I mess up, even being a half-vampire. I tell silly jokes to hide the fact that I'm a twenty-four-carat disappointment to everyone – including me.

I was actually closing my eyes, surrendering myself to my grisly fate, when a voice started whispering in my ear: *'Get up, Marcus. You've got to fight them for both of us.'*

I blinked and for one brilliant moment I thought Colin was back again. That energized me – until I realized he wasn't. It was only his voice I could somehow hear.

'Get up, Marcus,' he whispered again.

'Can't,' I whispered back. 'Can't even breathe.'

'But you're forgetting the power is inside you.'

I wished he'd stop saying that because it clearly wasn't. But his words seemed to dance round and round in my head: *The power is inside you. The power is inside you.*

'And there it's staying – despite all my hand-shaking,' I muttered.

Only Colin's words were so insistent that I couldn't help chanting them to myself as well. *'The power is inside me . . . The power is inside me.'* And more than anything I wanted that to be true.

The very next moment I had the strangest feeling. It was just as if I was in a lift which had rattled down forty floors at once. My stomach gave this absolutely massive lurch and I let out the world's largest burp – I tell you, the sound just ripped across the room.

My eyes sprang open. My hands weren't just tingling, they were spinning crazily. And then I felt this incredible surge of energy speeding through me.

My special powers were bursting out of me at last – and how. It was intoxicating and scary, both at once, because my head felt as if it was about to explode. But the very next moment it was filled with lightness. And this feeling came over me that I could do anything. Here I was in a stink-filled room, yet I was soaring now.

And before I knew it I was on my feet again

(I don't even remember getting up). Instantly, two more bats dived at me. I let out another mighty burp, yelled, 'Forgive my bad manners,' and dived away from their assault with breathtaking ease.

That was just a start, of course. More bats quickly lunged at me, but I jabbed them away without any real effort at all. And I was so quick, it was as if someone had sent me into fast forward. And soon I was diving about, sending bats sprawling right across the sitting room.

Hugo had been watching his army of bats like a proud ringmaster. Now shock and frustration raced across his face. And he fired another lightning bolt at me. The speed it travelled at was incredible. Normally I wouldn't have stood a chance of getting out of its way. But now I could vault away from it with ease. And as I did so I shouted, 'Hey, this is brilliant fun, so glad you all called round.'

That's when, far, far away, I thought I could hear Colin laughing. Somehow I knew he was still here with me.

The next moment a voice said very slowly

and with huge effort, 'I'm so proud of you, Marcus.'

I whirled round and there was my dad.

For the first time in his life Dad was proud of me. I had to take on a team of deadly vampires for that to happen, but it was still a terrific moment.

I gave Dad a quick wave and then the bats launched themselves towards me again. 'In the mood for some more fighting, are you?' I said. 'Well, that's good – so am I.'

I swung away from them so easily, I tell you, I could have done it blindfolded. Then I sent two bats spinning right across the room. 'Sorry to be so brutal,' I said, 'but your breath stinks. In fact, you lot all need to visit the dentist urgently – or at least suck some mints.'

Their teeth seemed different too, a horrible gungy-brown colour now. That could have given me a clue as to what was going to happen next.

But it didn't. It was a total shock.

CHAPTER THIRTY

Tuesday 6 January

6.05 p.m. (cont'd)

It happened very suddenly. I remember Dad struggling to shout out a warning to me.

I turned and quickly realized why. The largest bat was zigzagging across the room, one moment diving towards me, the next zooming right away.

Then all the other bats started doing exactly the same. What was going on now? Did Hugo have one last grim trick up his sleeve?

Then something even more incredible happened. The largest bat shot right up to the ceiling. It perched there, its red eyes bulging more horribly than ever. That's when I noticed what looked like thick white slime oozing out of both of its eyes.

After which it dived down from the ceiling, nearly touching the ground before whirling around maniacally like some demented firework. Was this some weird show of strength? What was going on?

But then the bat brought its show to a close by rupturing into thousands and thousands of pieces of dust. Bits splattered everywhere, flying all around the room. Before I could recover from that shock all the other bats started exploding all around us too.

'Change back! Change back!' yelled Hugo desperately. But they obviously couldn't. Instead, they followed the same pattern as the first bat, swirling round and round and then hovering in the air like targets in a shooting gallery. Moments later they exploded into thousands and thousands of pieces. And all that was left of them was dust flying everywhere and a very foul smell.

Dad began edging very slowly towards me. Mum was in the doorway too. She gave me a wave that was more like a salute. I felt like a knight riding into battle against a deadly army.

But actually there was only one member of the army left now – Hugo. 'What are you looking at, you useless half-vampire?' he snarled.

'We thought you'd like to know,' I said, 'that a funny liquid is now exiting out of your mouth.'

And it really was.

Weird yellow stuff was shooting out of his mouth and all over the room. Hugo suddenly let out this piercing scream. Smoke was now billowing out of him too. Then his whole body gave a terrible lurch and soon there was far more smoke than Hugo. The smoke circled and curled up into the air while Hugo's cape floated to the ground, joined by his hat – and finally his boots thumped down too. Seconds later, dust was fired once more into every corner of the room.

'What's happened to them all?' I asked Dad.

'I'm not exactly sure,' said Dad. There was a huge gap between each word he spoke, but at least he was speaking now. He continued, 'You did extremely well.'

'And all on your own,' added Mum slowly.

'Oh no, I wasn't on my own,' I said. 'In fact, I had the best help you could ask for.' I was thinking of Colin, but Dad thought I meant my special power.

'It's come through and you are a very, very rare half-vampire.' And Dad struggled to explain to me what a one-in-a-thousand half-vampire was. But he needed to save all his energy right now, so I interrupted and said Tara had told me all about it.

Then Mum started to cough so badly she nearly fell over. 'What are we doing standing in this stinky room?' I said. 'I'll make you both a cup of tea.'

The kettle had nearly boiled by the time they'd reached the kitchen. I tell you, an arthritic tortoise could have won a race with them right now. After I'd given them their tea Mum asked me to open all the windows in the sitting room. Icy cold air gushed in, but it would take a long time to get rid of the stale rotting stench that hung over everything. All the light seemed to have drained from the room too.

Then the doorbell rang. And a voice yelled, 'Let me in! This is urgent! It's Cyril.'

CHAPTER THIRTY-ONE

Tuesday 6 January

6.05 p.m. (cont'd)

I called out to my parents, 'Don't worry, I'll get rid of him.'

When I opened the door Cyril sprang forward, his face bright red. He stuttered, 'They tried to stop me getting here to warn you. They're on their way to—' Then he stopped and sniffed and his face grew even redder. 'They've been here already?'

'Yes.'

'Are you all right?'

'Never better, only my mum and dad were—'

But Cyril had already dashed past me and

dived into the sitting room, where he rushed around like a demented terrier. 'You've had a real infestation of vampires here. So where are they now?'

'Having a rest upstairs. I'm just making them a cup of tea, actually.'

Cyril was so worked up he was even believing me a tiny bit.

'No, they've been and gone,' I said airily.

I explained what had happened. Only I missed out the part about me fighting them all off. Much as I'd have liked Cyril to have known that, it would have aroused too much curiosity. So I let Cyril think they'd exploded almost as soon as they'd arrived. Then I asked him why the deadly vampires had all just turned to dust like that.

'Drinking all that human blood so quickly is something no vampire has ever tried before. And now it looks as though a fatal reaction has set in.'

'So their foul smell—'

'Oh yeah, that was a sign it was starting to affect them . . .'

'Which they tried to cover up with revolting aftershave.'

'But they were obsessed with all the new powers blood was giving them. In fact, it was all they could think about. So they ignored all the advice to cut back. Really, they were like bombs just waiting to explode.'

'Which they did all over our sitting room,' I said.

'It must have been quite a sight,' said Cyril. And he sounded positively envious to have missed it.

'And if they had been victorious here, they were going to do something in Great Walden to shock everybody. What was that?' I asked.

'I don't know for certain,' said Cyril, 'but I sense they planned to target that giant snowball fight, which is going on not very far from here right now.'

I was too stunned to breathe at first. That was the snowball fight Joel had told me about. I bet half of my school was there now.

'That snowball fight would have been the perfect opportunity for the vampires to attack. All those children outside providing easy targets . . .'

'That is shocking. I thought they'd attack the Town Hall or something, not people just innocently throwing snowballs at each other.'

'This would have been the deadly vampires' first big demonstration. Many more were planned.'

'But now they've gone for good?' I asked.

'No vampire will ever return to Great Walden, not after such a total humiliation. But here in your sitting room you might over the next few days catch a glimpse of a part of them. A stray hand, for instance, or one of their eyes might float through the air, just for a moment.'

'Lovely,' I said.

'But they can't do any harm, they're just the last remnants—' He stopped. Dad was tottering towards us. 'I was so sorry to hear about your ordeal,' said Cyril, rushing over to him.

'Oh, I am in perfect health,' said Dad. He was choking his words out, but still saying them very firmly, as if daring Cyril to argue with him. Dad went on, 'I know Marcus is a big fan of your stories. You must have a remarkable imagination.'

Dad's tone was genial, but Cyril actually flinched at the last two words.

Dad continued, 'Thank you so much for calling round, and if I don't see you again' – and Dad's tone suggested that he really didn't expect to – 'all the best for the future.'

Cyril was, in the nicest possible way, being ordered out of our house for ever. And although Cyril was nearly a head taller than my dad, right now he looked like a gangly schoolboy facing the headmaster.

Dad went on staring at Cyril for a moment and then it was as if some secret message had been passed between them. That's the only way I can describe it. And Dad visibly relaxed, while Cyril said, 'I shall actually be leaving Great Walden in a day or two, so I just came round to say goodbye to Marcus, really.'

'Well, that's extremely civil of you.' And Dad seemed positively friendly now as he said, 'Marcus will see you to the door. Goodbye and good luck.'

At the door I asked Cyril, 'Are you really leaving, then?'

'Nothing to stay for now,' said Cyril, 'especially as this is the very last place vampires will ever materialize in again.'

'So where are you going?'

'Well, Uncle Giles came out of hospital yesterday so we'll be going back to London, for a while at least. But first I must sincerely apologize to you for funking it.' He looked away. 'I wasn't really away consulting experts, you know.'

'I sort of guessed that, actually. So what were you doing?'

'Hiding!' He shouted the word, shaking his head at himself. And do you know, I never liked Cyril more than I did then.

'At least you're honest,' I said.

'I was hiding,' he said again, 'while Tallulah got attacked and you—'

'Come on, you did try and warn me today.'

'A feeble effort and far, far too late. No, I may have many talents but I am definitely not a man of action.' He frowned for a moment. 'Do give Tallulah my apologies and my very best. I sincerely hope she's out of hospital soon. She's a brave girl.'

'Yeah, she is.' Then I added, 'And I thought Dad would be much more bothered about you. But he seemed to just look at you and—' All at once I knew what Dad had seen. Of course! Of course! I was so excited I blurted out, 'You're one of us, aren't you?'

Cyril stepped back. 'I don't know what you mean.' But there was something at the edge of his lips that looked suspiciously like a smile.

'But you are, aren't you?' I hissed. 'Just nod your head a little.'

'I shall do no such thing,' said Cyril. But a smile was positively dancing on his lips now.

'So that night,' I said, 'when you questioned me about my relatives . . . ?'

'Just call it a little test which you passed with flying colours. But tampering with vampires' – he whispered the word – 'is especially dangerous for us. So I wanted you to be completely on your guard.' He went on, 'My interest in my distant, highly disreputable cousins is frowned upon by many in our community. So I'm an outsider, really. Uncle Giles – who is not, by the way, one of us – is my only ally. But I would never betray anyone.' Then he stretched out a hand. And to my great surprise I was rather sorry to see him go. 'Good luck, Marcus,' he said. 'I have no doubt you will continue to lead a most interesting life.'

Back inside, I said to Dad, 'So Cyril is—'

'Completely trustworthy,' interrupted Dad. Then he put his finger to his mouth. 'No more talk now,' he hissed.

So instead I asked Dad how he was feeling.

'Better all the time, your mother too. And we look forward to celebrating with our son, the one-in-a-thousand HV.'

'On a scale of one to ten, how shocked were you when you found out?'

'Eleven,' said Dad.

8.15 p.m.

Things I can now do.

Fly.

Fight brilliantly.

Send messages by telepathy to anyone.

Transform into a bat in less than a second.

Run fast.

And that's just a few of the highlights.

You might even say I've turned into Batman – only without the stupid costume.

So how about giving myself a new super-hero name?

I've got it: *Marcus, righter of wrongs and*

now *known throughout the universe as
Deadly Fists.*

Yeah, I like that.

8.20 p.m.

Got a real ring to it, don't you think – *Deadly
Fists*?

Personally, I prefer it to Batman or
Spider-Man.

10.15 p.m.

'So what's it like to have a superhero for a son?'
We've been toasting my new powers with a
glass of blood (actually, I've been allowed two).
My parents are practically back to normal.
Only we've had to spend the evening in the
kitchen as the sitting room still reeks. 'And are
you both a bit proud of me now?' I went on.

'We'd have been extremely proud of you if
you'd just achieved one special power – or had
no powers at all,' said Dad.

'You never have to prove yourself to us,'
added Mum.

Now they tell me!

'Those extra powers I've got are mine
for good now, aren't they?' I asked this quite

casually, but do you know what Dad replied?

'Well, yes – and no.'

What kind of answer was that?

And wouldn't you know, there's a catch? At the moment all my new powers will burst in and out of me. One minute they're there, the next they might start to slip away again. To be able to call them up whenever I need them – and to control them – I'll have to go away on a special training course in France. In Paris.

Only this won't be like the crash course I went on earlier. No. Much, much posher, apparently. And there are currently only three other half-vampires at this academy – that's how extremely rare having all these multi-powers is. But I need to be away for a couple of months. My parents will come with me – and they will make all the arrangements, including with my school. (Good luck with that one!)

But I don't *have* to go.

Both my parents emphasized this. If I don't go, I will still have 'untrained' special powers. I just won't have the expertise to make full use of them, that's all.

'In the past,' said Dad, 'maybe we've been a little over-eager. So that's why we want this to be completely your decision. And if you decide not to go to the academy and think you'd rather stay and concentrate on the human side of your life – you won't hear one word of complaint from us.'

'Can I have that in writing?' I said it just as a kind of joke really.

But my dad replied, 'You have our solemn promise on that one.'

11.50 p.m.

Everyone's gone to bed already – an insanely early time for half-vampires. But we're all shattered.

Just before I went upstairs I took one last peek inside the sitting room. None of us had gone near it all evening. It was very stinky and very gloomy.

And then I realized I was being watched. One very red eye was floating towards me, all by itself.

I nearly tore out of there, but Cyril had said this would happen, I told myself. And it couldn't harm me any more, could it? Only I wasn't sure the red eye knew that as it flew right up to me, blazing furiously.

Then it did two laps around the sitting room and vanished again.

Before I got over that shock I saw a skeletal hand clinging to the ceiling. The next moment it had dropped down and made straight for my throat, which it attempted to squeeze tightly.

I easily pushed it away.

'When will you get the message?' I said. 'I'm not playing with you any more – because I've won.' Then it fell off me, rolled onto the floor and vanished again.

And that was the end of tonight's special effects.

I left then, but didn't mention what had happened to my parents. They'd had enough shocks today.

But I saw again how those deadly vampires really had meant business today. And if my special powers hadn't come through when they did . . . well, they'd have seen me off very quickly and made straight for that snowball fight.

And I so very nearly gave up today. In fact, if it hadn't been for Colin . . .

I owe him plenty.

I only met him twice. But I know I'll remember him for ever.

CHAPTER THIRTY-TWO

Wednesday 7 January

9.30 a.m.

We've just rung Tallulah's parents – and Tallulah's taken a turn for the worse.

That one piece of news has totally wiped out all the brilliant stuff that happened yesterday. I don't even care that those deadly vampires have destroyed themselves.

None of that matters against Tallulah getting better.

11.15 a.m.

I've just been talking to Gracie. She thinks I should go and see Tallulah right now. So do I.

And I don't care what my parents say or how bad the roads still are.

12.30 p.m.

I thought my parents would try and talk me out of visiting Tallulah. But instead, the car's just been repaired and Dad's driving me to the hospital later this afternoon.

5.30 p.m.

I've seen Tallulah.

She was lying there with all these tubes sticking out of her and hardly moving at all. Her parents looked so drained, so defeated, I had to turn away from them. It was as if they'd totally given up on her.

Then the doctor bustled in and wanted to talk to Tallulah's parents for a moment. So they left – and my mum and dad got up too. I think they wanted to give me a moment alone with Tallulah. My last. No, I had to stop thinking like that.

It was just this horrible, antiseptic smell – nearly as grisly as the pong still lurking in our sitting room. It made everything seem so grim and hopeless. But there was so much I wanted to say to Tallulah. So I knelt down beside her and whispered, 'Tallulah, I hope you can hear me because we won yesterday. Do you understand what I mean?'

Did her eyes flicker the tiniest bit? Or was I just imagining it? Anyway, I went on whispering into her ear now, 'I put up a pretty good fight, if I say so myself. But all those DVs just blew themselves up – too much blood. Cyril was there too, and you should have been as well. After all, you were the brains of this outfit. Don't you always say that?'

It was surprisingly easy to talk to Tallulah like this. I suppose I never had to worry about what she'd say back. In a weird way it freed me up. So I went on, 'When you get better, we'll have a massive celebration. I can't wait for that. And I can't wait for you not to laugh at my jokes.' I moved closer. 'And don't ever think of leaving me because you mean the world to me. Did you hear that, Tallulah? You mean the world to me.'

I'd like to believe her eyes flickered then. I couldn't be completely sure.

But I think they did.

CHAPTER THIRTY-THREE

Wednesday 14 January

6.00 p.m.

A whole week has now gone by.

I tried to write a couple of times, but I couldn't. My whole life has just been on hold. And I haven't given a single thought as to whether I should go to that academy for special half-vampires.

Nothing has mattered, except today I got the news I've been hoping for so keenly. Tallulah is no longer at risk. She's still pretty frail and will have to go straight off to that sanatorium the second she leaves hospital.

But she's out of danger.

Gracie always believed Tallulah would get

through this and she's been proven completely right.

6.05 p.m.

So what else has happened?

Well, the snow's still hanging around, only it's gone all brown and slushy now. And that stench is still lurking in the sitting room, although it's much fainter. Mum's talking of having the room completely decorated. I haven't sighted any more floating vampire parts, but I've hardly gone in there really.

As for my special powers – yeah, they're still twisting about. I had this mock fight with my dad last night. He was amazed at how strong I was. And you should see me literally flying up and down the stairs – brilliant. My parents have made me promise I'll never fly outside in the daytime. As if I would! Although I'd love to see our neighbours' faces if they suddenly saw me skimming past their window!

Even better would be to fly out of one of our school assemblies. Just as the headmaster was moaning on about school uniform again, off I'd float.

The special powers do come and go, though.

And I suppose it would be good to be able to control them. But do I really want to go away for two whole months? Shouldn't I just settle down here for a while now?

Saturday 17 January

I visited Tallulah in hospital today.

She still looked pretty awful – her cheeks have sunk right in. But it was great to talk to her. And she seemed pleased to see me. We couldn't say much, though, as she had some relatives visiting too ('I don't know why,' she hissed, 'because they all hate me, and I hate them') and they hovered around us the whole time.

I was amazed at all the cards Tallulah had received. There were even ones from Joel and Gracie. 'And I just met Gracie once,' said Tallulah, 'so thank her for me.'

As I was leaving I said, 'Well, I'll see you again soon – if not sooner.'

Tallulah just nodded and smiled faintly.

Monday 19 January

Tallulah came out of hospital this afternoon

but was sent straight off to the sanatorium. That's rough. She so deserves something brilliant to happen to her now.

I think about her a lot, but I can't see us ever going out together. The very idea seems crazy now.

Tuesday 20 January

I've finally reached a decision about that academy for half-vampires.

The first time I thought about it I wasn't sure. And the second . . . and . . . well, you get the idea. But strangely I woke up today with my mind completely clear. I just knew I had to go to Paris.

It's got nothing to do with my parents either. I could have gone on with my normal life without any hassle from them. But I don't want to. You could say I live in two worlds now. And right now an opportunity has turned up in the half-vampire part. And that's a big part of me. So I'd be mad not to take it really, wouldn't I?

Wednesday 21 January

Things are now moving insanely fast. I'm off on the Eurostar to Paris with my parents this Friday. Dad has told the school that he's over there on business for a while, so I will go to school there while we all have to be in France. Actually, I'll only see my parents on Sunday afternoons, so it's a bit like going away to boarding school, which I'm not mad about.

But it'll be the world's smallest boarding school. And my parents did say if I'm not happy I can just leave. Shame they never said that about my normal school.

Thursday 22 January

Gracie came round tonight. 'The first time you can be seen in all your glorious non-hairiness,' I said, 'and I go away tomorrow. Not great timing, is it?'

'Totally lousy,' she agreed.

'Still, you could always come with me. Yeah, be a stowaway.'

'I'd love to go to Paris,' she said, 'but I'm not a one-in-a-thousand.'

'But you are the girlfriend of a one-in-a-thousand. You are my girlfriend now, aren't you?'

'No.'

'Would you like to reconsider that answer?'

'No.'

I was shocked.

'But you and I belong together. We're like bacon and eggs and fish and chips – Gracie 'n' Marcus. See, I even gave you top billing. So, come on, what's going on here?'

Gracie didn't answer. Instead, she hugged me. Then she said, 'If you ask me again when you get back . . . ?'

'If I ask you . . .'

'Well, then I'll definitely say yes.'

I still didn't understand why she couldn't say 'yes' now. But I suppose that's girls for you – always having to make a drama out of everything.

Friday 23 January

6.30 a.m.

This is it, then. My very last hours in Great Walden, for two months. I'll be in Paris early this afternoon. And yeah, nerves are kicking in a bit now.

Inevitable, I suppose.

I'm still not sure what's going to happen to me next. But there are times when I find myself smiling for no reason at all, as if somewhere deep inside me I'm happy.

And I suppose I am. Well, I'm following my destiny. That sounds very grand, doesn't it? Not like me at all. Except 'me' keeps changing. Well, some of me does. That's why I really hated being a half-vampire at first. There were so many changes it felt as if I'd been dropped into a story which had nothing to do with me.

But I don't feel like that at all now. Tara's right: weird is good – brilliant, in fact. And bubbling up inside me is the feeling that going to this academy might just count as one of the great decisions of my life.

I'd like to come back and tell you about it one day.

But for now – well, this feels like an ending, doesn't it?

It *is* an ending.

Hey, I'm choking up now. Can't have that.

So before I go I shall leave you with a few words of wisdom to remember me by. I'm going to tell you the two things that make for a brilliant blog.

And the first is – always leave the reader wanting more.

BYE!

READ AND DESTROY

Hi, Marcus,

I don't think I've ever written a letter to anyone before except to thank some ancient crone for sending me a handkerchief which I immediately threw away.

So here it is – my first proper letter to anyone. It was all Gracie's idea, and she's going to forward this on to you at your school in Paris, which I hope isn't too gruesome.

Yeah, I'm still at the fun palace(!) and hating every millisecond. The only thing which has kept me sane is remembering how we saw off those deadly vampires and how there's a whole secret world out there which hardly anyone - except for us, Cyril and Giles - knows about.

By the way, I loved working with you on our missions. I know I might not have always shown it, but I did.

But when you asked me out on the ghost train, well, it changed everything. You pushed me back into the real world again, which I'd spent every minute of my time avoiding.

And at first I really didn't think I could cope with that. So I panicked - and I know I expressed myself so badly to you then. But the very next night I did come looking for you to apologize - and that was before I had a hint, or imagined I did, about you possibly having secret relatives.

But I don't want to go over all that old stuff again as I have a shocking new secret to tell you. Are you ready for this?

I have gone off vampires.

I suppose when a whole pack of them try to drain you of all the blood you possess it does make you re-think just why you like them so much.

But actually, it's something Cyril said about them. Remember when he said they didn't have any heart and I said, 'Cool'?

Even then I didn't really mean it. I was just – showing off, I suppose. But not to care about anyone, ever, I know I don't want to be like that.

And I'm not.

There is someone who means the world to me. Oh yeah, I heard every word you said to me that day in hospital, and maybe you just said it because you thought I was about to snuff it. But I care about you too, Marcus. I care about you a lot.

What a totally embarrassing letter, I know. So I'm stopping now.

But I will get out of here. And if you're

waiting for me at Great Walden when I do –
well, I can't think of anything in the world more
brilliant than that.

Love,

Tallulah